Adachi and Shimamura

STORY BY **Hitoma Iruma** ART BY **Non**

NOVEL **4**

"Want to eat lunch together? You're Shimamura-san, right?"

"Yep, that's me."

"Care to join us? Or do you have plans with someone?"

"Nope, no plans."

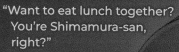

Shimamura

A girl with a bit of a ditzy side. Used to have bleached hair, but she dyed it back to her natural color. She wears more makeup than Adachi does, but sees Adachi as the more beautiful of the two.

"Hey, um, wait. You dropped this."

"Oh, thanks... Oh! Oh my god! Thank you so much!"

Adachi

She has a slim, stick-figure body type with few curves to speak of. Has feelings for Shimamura, but they haven't been able to hang out in a while, and it's tearing her apart.

"Isn't that kind
of a lot?"
"You can have
some if you
want."

We spent Christmas together.

We exchanged chocolates on Valentine's Day.

I was so sure we'd stay together during our second year, too. What can I do to get her back? Should I look for a new place for us? Somewhere she'd like?

Table of Contents

Adachi and Shimamura

NOVEL 4

STORY BY
Hitoma Iruma

ILLUSTRATED BY
Non

Seven Seas Entertainment

ADACHI TO SHIMAMURA VOL. 4

© Hitoma Iruma 2015
Edited by Dengeki Bunko
Illustrations by Non

First published in Japan in 2015 by
KADOKAWA CORPORATION, Tokyo.
English translation rights arranged with
KADOKAWA CORPORATION, Tokyo.

Seven Seas press and purchase enquiries can be sent to
Marketing Manager Lianne Sentar at press@gomanga.com.
Information regarding the distribution and purchase of
digital editions is available from Digital Manager CK Russell
at digital@gomanga.com.

Follow Seven Seas Entertainment online at
sevenseasentertainment.com.

TRANSLATION: Molly Lee
COVER DESIGN: Nicky Lim
LOGO DESIGN: George Panella
INTERIOR LAYOUT & DESIGN: Clay Gardner
PROOFREADER: Nino Cipri, Stephanie Cohen
LIGHT NOVEL EDITOR: Nibedita Sen
PREPRESS TECHNICIAN: Rhiannon Rasmussen-Silverstein
PRODUCTION MANAGER: Lissa Pattillo
MANAGING EDITOR: Julie Davis
ASSOCIATE PUBLISHER: Adam Arnold
PUBLISHER: Jason DeAngelis

ISBN: 978-1-64505-720-8
Printed in Canada
First Printing: February 2021
10 9 8 7 6 5 4 3 2 1

1. Sakura and Spring

AS I PEERED SURREPTITIOUSLY at Sakura-san's face, sure enough, it seemed to be crafted out of ice, just as everyone always said. Her eyes were empty mirrors, merely reflecting what was in front of her, no curiosity burning within.

It was spring, and we had just started our final year of junior high. As a result of my utter lack of assertiveness, I ended up assigned as a library helper. The official title was "Cultural Events Committee" or something to that effect, but our only real task was to sit around in the library. Hence, library helper. And today was our first day on the job.

The two of us were seated at the front counter, side by side, and admittedly, I was nervous. Sakura-san and I were in the same class last year as well, but I'd never spoken to her. Still, even from a distance I could tell what sort of person she was: cold, distant, quiet...and beautiful. At last, I finally understood why people likened her to an ice sculpture.

But of course, I couldn't just sit here and admire her all day long. So I took a deep breath and summoned all my courage.

"Um...?"

Feebly, I called out to her, and the distant look in her eyes grew sharp once more.

"...What?"

A beat later, she turned to look at me, fixing me with those glossy, uninterested eyes at point-blank range. Once again, I got the sense that she honestly couldn't care less about the people around her. It was probably a miracle that she was sitting here at all. What about our next shift? Would she even show up? Maybe if it was during lunch, like today, but something told me she wouldn't stick around after school.

"Uh, your job...? The checkout card...?"

There was a girl standing literally right in front of her at the counter, trying to check out a book. She'd been there for quite some time now. But Sakura-san never seemed to notice her; thus, I had no choice but to intervene.

"Oh, right." She didn't bat a lash. Instead, she handled the girl's checkout card at her own pace.

The girl in question put a hand on her hip like she was ready to give her a piece of her mind...but Sakura-san didn't seem to notice *that*, either. Before the girl could find an opportunity to speak up, however, Sakura-san finished her half of the process and handed the checkout card back to its owner. Reluctantly, the girl bent over to write in her name and date. Gazing at the girl's scalp, Sakura-san mumbled:

"...Sorry for the wait."

At first, the girl didn't realize the words were directed at her. By the time she looked up, however, Sakura-san had already averted her gaze.

"Uh...no problem," the girl shrugged.

Meanwhile, I sat there in stunned silence. *She apologized!* I always thought she was too stuck-up, so this rare moment of humility caught me by surprise. But Sakura-san didn't seem to feel too guilty about slacking off on the clock, because she went right back to spacing out... and I went right back to admiring her face in profile.

She was like this in class, too. She never spoke with anyone, never went anywhere with anyone. But she wasn't isolated against her will; rather, she seemed to choose the loner life of her own volition. This was evidenced by the fact that she was never bullied or harassed, possibly because she had the sort of aura that suggested she'd clap back without batting an eye. Thus, everyone tended to avoid her...including me.

But now, my eyes were drawn to her. After all, this was a rare opportunity to get a closer look at something I could normally never approach.

Sakura-san had quite a few admirers, male and female, but no one ever reached out. They could look, but they couldn't touch. After all, she was an ice sculpture—cold, sharp, and fragile.

Sure enough, Sakura-san didn't come back for library duty the next day, probably because it was an after-school shift. As for me, I was far from pleased that my prediction was accurate. At the counter, I sat on the edge of my chair and contemplated what to do. *Should I sit here, or should I go look for her?* Was she even still on campus?

After a moment of debate in which I rose to my feet and sat back down several times in a row, I ultimately decided to go look for her. After all, the bell had only just rung, so chances were high she was still at her shoe locker.

To reduce the amount of time the library would be left unattended, I broke into a run as soon as I hit the hallway.

Then I flew down the stairs. How long had it been since I ran this fast? It would've been autumn at the very least; winter had a way of making exercise uniquely miserable. Perhaps this was proof that spring had sprung.

Right as my legs went into high gear, I spotted her at last, pulling her outdoor shoes out of her locker. As I ran up to her, she glanced over at me, but only briefly. Evidently she didn't realize my business was with her.

"Hold it right there!" I shouted as I closed in.

At last, Sakura-san realized she was my target. She turned back, annoyed. My heart fluttered in my chest.

"We have library duty today! Remember?"

"Oh...right."

Apparently she had simply forgotten about it. Her gazed flickered between me and her locker. Then she nodded to herself, and...set off for the front entrance.

"Wh... Hey, hey, hey! I don't think so!"

Timidly, I grabbed her sleeve. She didn't shake me off, but the look on her face was far from enthusiastic. Not a trace of motivation to be seen.

"Do you really need two people for that job?"

In terms of excuses, unfortunately, this was actually a good one. The library lines were never very long, and the fact of the matter was, I could probably handle it myself just fine. After all, Sakura-san had barely lifted a finger last time. Still, I couldn't accept it. Without her there, there wasn't much for me to look forward to...

"Maybe not, but...it's still your job!"

With no other solid argument, I was forced to appeal to her integrity.

She seemed to have trouble thinking of a counter-argument, because she reluctantly returned her outdoor shoes to her locker. Once again, as with the apology from yesterday, this was more evidence that she was, in fact, a sensible person. Granted, this ran counter to her reputation, but...maybe she was more normal than people made her out to be.

Once she changed back into her indoor shoes, we set off down the hallway, and I gazed down at my hand—at the fingers that had touched Sakura-san (technically just her clothes, but still). They were still faintly pink, with no sign of frostbite.

Arriving back at the library, Sakura-san took her seat at the counter without any fuss. Then, as with last time, she stared off into the distance, yawning occasionally. Was she sleepy, or just bored? She could always read books to pass the time like I did, and yet she chose not to. What was on her mind while she sat there perfectly still? Was she wishing her shift would hurry up and end already?

She was an enigma, and I found myself intrigued.

"Do you like to read?" I asked, after I gathered a bit of courage.

"If it's a book I like, then sure, I'll read it," she answered, her chin propped up on her elbow. It was a vague answer, probably because Sakura-san didn't really care whether I understood.

Hoping to get to know her, I summoned what little courage I had left and offered: "Would you like me to recommend you some of my favorites?"

Unfortunately...

"Huh? No, I'll pass." She waved her hand to dismiss the idea. Then she turned back and stared straight ahead once more.

I was appalled. She shot me down point-blank, no sugar-coating. And yet...she didn't seem annoyed with me, either. Her tone was flat—bland and flavorless, like she sincerely wasn't interested. But that only intrigued me more.

I snuck a furtive glance at her face. Surely there had to be *something* Sakura-san would take an interest in... but what?

I never imagined being a library helper would be so thought-provoking. I could scarcely concentrate on the book in my hands. Instead, I searched and searched for some sort of common ground with Sakura-san. Not that I really expected to find any.

Her expression was like perfectly polished ice, its chill keeping everyone at bay. And if she wasn't going to meet me halfway, then I was going to have to be the one to reach out. The best way to get to know someone? Conversation.

"So, um...what do you like to do on weekends?"

"Nothing much. Sleep. Lay around in bed."

Aren't those the same thing?

She didn't seem to be lying, though. But while I appreciated her honesty, it wasn't very helpful for my purposes.

"Okay, umm... Do you get good grades, usually?"

"Just average."

"Oh, okay... Cool..."

At least she was willing to answer my questions. It would have been far worse if she ignored me outright... although this wasn't much better. At the rate I was headed, I'd never strike upon any common ground. I needed to take this a step further. Could I break through that icy exterior? Or would I slip and fall on my face?

As I contemplated my next move, my vision grew hazy and distant. And as I hung my head, the words fell from my lips like swollen tears.

"Do you...have any friends?"

"No," she replied flatly, without a single second of hesitation.

Her answer overwhelmed me all at once, like an

avalanche. My fingers started to tremble as they clutched the edges of my book. "That sucks."

"Yeah."

In that case...

My throat quavered.

Would you want to be friends with me?

I wanted to say it. I tried to say it. But the words wouldn't come.

I had plenty of friends here at school, but not once had I ever *asked* someone to be friends with me outright, like I was formally applying for the position. In an instant, I was overcome with shame and fear of rejection, and I needed some time to fight through it.

If only I could have said it faster, maybe things would have played out differently.

Instead, Sakura-san stared straight ahead and muttered, "But I'm fine with it."

The ice was smooth, transparent, cold, and hard... without a single crack. And the sight of it chased away the question on the tip of my tongue.

"I see," I muttered in kind.

She offered no reply to this, and for the first time, I accepted defeat.

After that, I went back to just looking at her. I didn't try to make conversation with her. And on the days she forgot about library duty, I didn't chase after her. To her credit, however, she turned up for the majority of our shifts. And as for me, I spent that time admiring her face in profile while pretending to read a book. Because I knew that was the most I could ever ask for.

Each time I gazed at her pretty pink lips, I was wracked with guilt. Deep down, I felt like I had failed her somehow. But that failure never stopped me from appreciating her beauty.

With the arrival of the second semester came a shuffling of job assignments, and my one tenuous connection to Sakura-san was unceremoniously severed. We were still classmates, of course, but I could never find the opportunity to go and talk to her. Plus, she was often absent, particularly on days that involved a lot of hassle.

And so nothing ever brought us together again for the rest of the year, right up to the day of our graduation. I half-wondered if she'd skip the ceremony, too, but fortunately she didn't. Honestly, she probably didn't even remember me. So I gazed at her from afar.

She stood at the front of the line, looking bored and uncomfortable, her head swaying to and fro. Once the principal's speech came to an end, the procession would start moving, and I'd lose sight of her...so for the first time in my life, I prayed that his dull rambling would never cease.

At the end of the ceremony, we all broke off into our own groups. Some left the gym, while others stayed behind. Following my intuition, I strayed away from my circle of friends and walked outside.

At the center of the school grounds was a single sakura tree, its blooms yet faintly budding. For now, spring was still just a whisper on the wind. As I gazed at the tiny specks of pink in the distance, I spotted a retreating figure I recognized. Instantly, my legs moved on autopilot, and I broke into a run.

"Sakura-san!" I called as I chased after her.

She slowly turned back to look at me. Even now, under the first rays of spring sun, her ice was unmelted. But her expression shifted slightly. Maybe she still recognized me after all.

"What's up?"

Sakura-san was prepared to walk off campus without saying goodbye to a single soul. This was the girl I had spent the past year admiring. And for some reason, I found I was delighted to have one more chilly moment with her.

"I, um...I wish you well... No, I mean, uh..."

Was that really all I wanted to say? This was my last chance. It was now or never. All at once, I was filled with reckless courage, or desperation, or whatever you want to call it. Regardless, I spurred myself forward.

Even if my message didn't land, I still wanted to put it out there.

"Thank you."

Her eyes narrowed in confusion, as if to ask *what for?* The answer, of course, was for letting me observe her during her most unguarded moments. For filling my days with something worthwhile. But even if I explained it to her in depth, I got the feeling it wouldn't resonate with her. She didn't need all the details. So instead, I smiled.

She stared at me dubiously for a moment, but eventually offered me a cold, curt "Glad it's over." A disinterested token response.

A sharp chill pierced my chest. *Yeah...I'm glad, too,* I answered silently. Then she walked off without so much as a goodbye.

Surrounded by cheers and laughter, I watched her go... and as the minutes ticked by, lukewarm water dripped down my torso as the ice in my chest started to melt.

In the future, if I ever encountered Sakura-san on the street, we probably wouldn't say a word to each other. That was why I chose to thank her.

Like a petal on the breeze, she vanished into a horizon as pink as her namesake…without ever looking back.

"Wait… Your first name is Sakura?"

"Yep."

Adachi started this conversation after the opening ceremony, as we left the school building. But she wasn't looking up at the blossoms overhead—no, she was looking at the dirty petals trampled into the ground below. Kind of depressing, actually. I tried my best to avoid walking on any and ended up staggering to and fro like a sloppy drunk.

"Did you mention that before?"

"Probably," Adachi nodded.

When was that? Back in the gym loft when we first met? I couldn't remember.

"I see… Well then," I muttered vaguely to fill the silence as I looked at the gym in the distance.

During the winter, the gym floor was practically ice, but I noticed it wasn't that bad during the ceremony today. As the sun's rays grew stronger, the loft would steadily become more and more appealing. Granted, all we could really do up there was sit in perfect silence like a couple of meditating monks, but it was still an escape. I glanced furtively at Adachi, wondering if perhaps we had outgrown our old hiding place...but wasn't especially encouraged by the look on her face.

Then it occurred to me: it still hadn't been a full year since we met. Hard to believe, I know. When I stopped to think about my friendship with her, it felt like I'd known her all my life, but at the same time, it *also* kinda felt like she might disappear one day. Perhaps our foundation was shaky...but if so, I wasn't really sure how to, you know, firm it up or whatever. *Hmm.*

"Sakura-chan!" I called, mostly as a joke.

At first, Adachi didn't react whatsoever...but when she realized I meant her, she whipped around and looked at me, her eyes as wide as saucers. I laughed and shrugged, and her whole face flushed pink, from her cheeks to her ears to her neck. A fitting color for a Sakura.

"Or would you prefer Sakura-san?" I teased.

At this, her shoulders began to shake, causing her hair to flop around like dog ears. It was kind of cute, actually. She seemed to need some time to recover, so I stared straight ahead and waited. Then, once the flopping sound stopped, I glanced back over—

"Hmm?"

She was grinning. A big, toothy grin, too, like she was only barely suppressing her weird giggling. This wasn't an expression I was aware she was capable of, so I peered at her curiously for a moment. Then she snapped back to her senses and looked up like she'd sensed my gaze. Her smile vanished, and her pink cheeks turned scarlet.

"Wh-what?" Adachi asked, readjusting her grip on her bookbag a dozen times as her eyes darted in all directions. Given her relative composure, maybe she wasn't aware she was grinning like a goof just now. If I told her about it, she'd probably flip out... I debated it for a few seconds, then decided to keep it to myself. After all, it'd be a real hassle to chase her down if she tried to bolt.

"Nothing. I was just looking at you," I lied.

She recoiled, bug-eyed. Then her gaze started to dart around again. *What's so weird about what I said?*

"Oh...huh... So you were... Okay then..."

This time her smile was stiff, like she was forcing it too hard. Now her eyes and mouth were all shaped like apple slices. It was painful to look at.

We passed through the school gates, and as we walked alongside the farm fields, in the back of my mind, something felt vaguely off.

Then I realized: it was Adachi's presence.

"Why are you following me?" I asked.

She froze, looking at me with puppy-dog eyes, like I'd hurt her feelings. This, in turn, alarmed me. *What's the matter?*

"Didn't you bring your bike today?" I pressed.

The bike parking area was, obviously, on school grounds. Not only that, but she lived in the opposite direction from me. So why was she still walking with me? Where was she going?

"Oh, *that's* what you meant?" Her eyes and mouth softened, like the binds holding them in place had come undone. She seemed relieved to hear it. But I was confused—what else could I have possibly meant?

She hadn't smiled even once during the opening ceremony, so I was worried she was having a bad day, but maybe not.

Today marked the start of our second year of high school, and the seating arrangement was currently in alphabetical order by last name, so Adachi was positioned diagonally to my left. I had chatted briefly with the new classmates seated around me, but Adachi hadn't spoken to anyone at all. Occasionally she would glance over at me, then look down at the floor, but that was about it. She just sat there, like she was waiting for time to tick by. Then, once the bell rang, she made a beeline right to me, reminiscent of my little sister.

While part of me was inclined to laugh and say "That's Adachi for you," another part of me was starting to get concerned. Not that I had any right to try to act like an older sister to someone my own age, but I couldn't help it. At this rate, she wasn't going to fit in with the rest of our new second-year class... Then again, if you asked me whether she "fit in" in our *last* class, the answer was a resounding *no*.

Ultimately, this was probably just...the sort of girl she was. But once she opened up to you, you quickly realized there was more to her than met the eye...and she had *really* opened up to me.

"Shimamura?"

"You really enjoy using that puppy-dog look on me, don't you?" I commented, casually leaving out the "pathetic" adjective I had in mind.

"What? I don't have a *puppy-dog look*," Adachi objected, patting her nose and cheeks. She seemed to take offense to the mere idea.

Maybe she didn't like dogs. But I did.

So, uh...is this the part where you turn around and go home? Because if you keep following me, you're gonna end up at my house.

But I had lost my opportunity to point this out, and so the two of us kept walking through the petals.

With the spring sun at my back, I quietly let out a breath.

interlude

A Visit to the Hino Estate
PART 1

AFTER SCHOOL ON FRIDAY, Nagafuji told me she wanted to hang out at my house.

I scowled. "Please, no."

"It's been two years... No, three years... Come to think of it, what did I have for dinner three nights ago? Hmmm..."

See? What'd I tell you? You can't trust your own memory! Just trust me instead! But she didn't seem to pick up on this, so I gave up. Instead, we kept walking, following the stone walkway out of the residential district...and that was how Nagafuji ended up at my house.

"It's like a summer home. I like it," she commented as she gazed up at the exterior.

"You think so?" I tilted my head. When I heard the words "summer home," I pictured a neat and tidy

Western-style building, not a Japanese mansion with a giant yard, overgrown trees, and a turtle infestation. "What part of this says 'summer home' to you?"

"The stone walkways...the pond...the smell of the trees...all of it," Nagafuji explained dutifully, pointing around at each in turn. Her nostrils flared up like she was trying to vacuum with her nose. *Chill.*

That said, she was right; it did smell pretty earthy out here. The residential district was surrounded with greenery to an unnatural degree, and trees were plentiful. It all reeked of old age. They'd remodeled the place several times in the past, but chose to leave the dreary old walls intact instead of rebuilding the house from scratch. The whole family lived here, including my grandfather, who often roped me into tea ceremonies held inside the tea house right next door. Suffice it to say, I wasn't a fan.

"I'll never get over how huge this place is."

"It's not even that big. It's just *wide*, that's all."

As I opened the door, the housemaid looked up from her shoe-polishing and smiled. "Welcome home."

"Yep! Glad to be back!"

Deep down, I was embarrassed to have anyone from school, even Nagafuji, witness what my home life was like. It was just too...*grandiose*. Ever since I was a kid, whenever I brought a friend over to hang out, I'd always get this weird feeling in my chest... It was impossible to describe.

"Thanks for having me!" Nagafuji declared. Speaking of *chests*, hers was making a declaration of its own. *Nagafuji's Meats, indeed. Where did I go wrong?*

"Is this a client...? No, a schoolmate?"

"She's a *friend*, alright? Just a friend." *No need to get all ceremonious about it. It's not a big deal. She's not the one paying your salary, anyway.*

"I'll have tea prepared at once."

"Oh, no, that's not necessary." *It's just Nagafuji.*

"Not to worry. I'm all set," Nagafuji announced, pulling out a half-empty bottle from a vending machine.

You know you bought that like four hours ago, right? It's not even cold by now.

The housemaid looked at the contents swaying within and smiled stiffly.

"See? She's fine. Don't worry about her," I told the maid as I pushed Nagafuji down the hall.

The hardwood flooring was so carefully polished, it was easy to slip and fall if you weren't careful. No amount of past experience would keep you safe, either.

Near the front entrance, the hallway branched off. Walking straight ahead would take you deeper into the house, while making a right turn would take you down

the outdoor walkway for a full view of the inner courtyard. Incidentally, the room immediately on the left
was my grandmother's; she often joked that she and my
grandfather were legally separated.

To get to my room, it was faster to cut through the
courtyard, so we made a right turn. Nagafuji followed
along after me, peering curiously at the walls and ceiling.
Then, a few steps later, I encountered a familiar face I
hadn't seen in a while.

"Ugh."

I had inadvertently run straight into my older brother
Goushirou, the fourth son of the family, wearing his tra-
ditional kimono. He looked at me and narrowed his eyes.

"That's no way to say hello to me, Akira."

He used to live here up until about two years ago,
so he was the brother I saw the most. Our relationship
wasn't hostile, but it wasn't comfortable, either. He was
always a bit of a nag.

"Rare to see you with a friend." He smiled slightly.

"She decided to follow me home, that's all."

"Greetings and hello!" Nagafuji called out from behind me. *Pick one of those and commit to it, damn it.*

"I'm Akira's older brother Goushirou," he replied.
Then he bowed deeply and solemnly, like a moron. Had
he never met Nagafuji before now?

"I am Nagafuji of Nagafuji's Meats."

Spare us the act, for the love of god. She tended to look intelligent on the outside, which meant he was going to think she was actually sensible and well-mannered.

"I hope you'll continue to guide and encourage our Akira."

"Oh, certainly. I'll whip her right into shape."

Cringe. Nagafuji might have been joking, but Goushirou most certainly wasn't. Why on earth would someone my age need to "guide and encourage" me, exactly?

He straightened back up and fixed me with a hard look. "We're entertaining some important guests today, so I must ask you not to make too much noise."

"Fine, fine. You go have fun with that." I waved at him and walked off. How did we end up with such wildly different personalities when we both grew up in the exact same house? He was such a hardass, you'd think we found him under a rock as a baby.

"Gosh, that guy was like a perfect clone of you!"

"No, he isn't. We're nothing alike."

My brothers were all very tall. When I was little, it felt like having five dads.

As we walked along past the courtyard, I ruminated on my brother's words. Important guests at the house... Hopefully they wouldn't try to drag me into it.

"Right! That's right!"

I heard the sound of Nagafuji clapping her hands together, so I turned to look at her. "'Sup?"

"I forgot your name was Akira!"

Oh, sure, NOW you remember. Probably because Goushirou said it out loud. Don't you remember when you used to chase me around shouting "Akira-chan"? How could you manage to forget?

And yet she somehow still got good grades in school. It was a total mystery to me how her brain functioned.

"What are your brothers' names again?"

As if you'll actually remember later, I thought to myself, but answered anyway: "The oldest is Kaiichirou, followed by Tokujirou, then Matasaburou, and lastly, Goushirou. That's the one you just met."

Each of their names contained the corresponding *kanji* for "one," "two," "three," and "four," in that order, so it was pretty easy for most people to remember. Fun fact: if I was born a boy, they would have named me Daigorou, with the *kanji* for "five." However, my father was overjoyed to have a daughter in the family, since it meant their compiled list of potential girl names hadn't gone to waste. Or so I was told.

"I see, I see," Nagafuji nodded, with a look on her face that told me she'd already forgotten them. "Well, I guess the only name I *really* need to remember is Hino."

"True."

A smart call, especially for her. Not like she'd ever be in the same room with my other brothers. And besides, even if she *did* try to memorize their names, she'd probably forget all about it after a day or two...but hey, at least she still remembered who I was after I came home from my overseas trip a while back.

We walked all the way to the room on the far corner; I slid the door open, and we entered my bedroom. The first thing Nagafuji did was take off her glasses and set them on the desk along with her bookbag. Then she flopped down on the tatami floor and started rolling around for some reason. I watched her, puzzled.

"Are you enjoying yourself down there?"

"Mostly I'm enjoying the smell of the tatami." Sure enough, she was flaring her nostrils again. "Your bedroom's bigger than my whole house!"

"It's just wider, that's all. Your house is taller."

Seriously, three whole floors! I enjoyed being way up high, so I was pretty jealous.

As she rolled, Nagafuji seemed to revel in the moment. Me personally, I was more worried that she might crush her boobs if she kept that up. *Doesn't it hurt? And for that matter, why doesn't it hurt when I do it? This is injustice!*

Then she came to a stop near the far wall. Lying flat on her back, she used her feet to push herself toward me a bit at a time, like a caterpillar, until she slid right between my legs. Was she trying to look up my skirt?! Reflexively, I jumped backwards. Not that she'd never seen my panties before, but at the same time, I didn't exactly want her looking at them, either.

Nagafuji looked up at me from the floor, tilting her head. "Aren't you going to get changed?"

"Say wha?"

"Into your kimono!" She swayed her arms as if to swing her imaginary kimono sleeves. Her boobs swayed, too.

"I don't wear that thing for fun, you know," I scoffed. Surely she knew I didn't lounge around the house in it.

"But you still wear it."

"I mean, yeah..."

She continued to swing her "sleeves" around, and her boobs... Well, you get the idea. She was being unusually stubborn about this, which could only mean one thing...

"...You want to see me wear it?"

"Wear it, wear it!"

She clapped her hands together like a little sea otter. I stood there and watched her. She kept clapping. Then I remembered that my brother had warned me to keep it down.

"Ugh, what a hassle."

Nevertheless, I flagged down a passing housemaid and asked her to fetch me a kimono. She offered to escort me to the changing room to help me put it on, but I declined. I didn't need *anyone's* help to put the damn thing on, and I didn't like the idea of her and Nagafuji both fussing over me. I couldn't stand people contrasting my home life with my school life.

I stripped off my school uniform, and as my skirt hit the floor, I turned back to find Nagafuji looking at me. "What?" she asked, gazing up at me with fuzzy eyes, as though she was playing innocent.

"What do you mean, 'what'? Quit looking at my butt."

"I can't help it."

"That's a lie and you know it."

"I don't look at anyone else's, you know."

"Uh...I mean, I figured, but..."

What did she mean by that? Was she just speaking in general, or was she trying to make a specific point? Both possibilities seemed correct. But either way, it was still rude to ogle my body. Or was there something about my butt that drew her interest? I kinda wanted to ask, but on the other hand, I didn't want to know.

As I pulled on my *nagajuban*, then my kimono over it, Nagafuji commented: "You're very adept at it."

"Well, yeah. I was formally trained."

"You remind me of a sales clerk wrapping up my purchase."

I wasn't sure if that was supposed to be a compliment or what. Nagafuji was a mystery I always struggled to decipher.

As I got dressed, I could feel her gaze on me at every moment. *Is it really that interesting to watch someone get changed? No, seriously, is it?* I could feel myself start to rush as I tied my *obi*. Then, at last, I was finished.

"There. Are you happy now?"

I swayed my sleeves at her; she reached up from the floor like a lazybones and tried to grab them, but missed. I stepped back, willing her to give chase, and she sprang up from the ground. Then, as I was having fun luring her along, she suddenly put a hand on my shoulder...and while I was distracted looking at it, she moved in front of me and pressed her lips to my forehead.

My eyes nearly popped out of my skull, but I quickly recovered. "The heck was that for?" I wasn't expecting it, but at the same time, I wasn't that surprised by it, either. Now there was a wet spot on my forehead.

With her hand still on my shoulder, Nagafuji looked squarely into my eyes and declared, "You're cute, Hino."

"Wh...where'd *that* come from?" I stammered, flummoxed. I never knew how to handle plain, direct compliments like hers.

"It's an observation I made just now," she replied, gazing unflinchingly into my eyes. Her shadow fell over me, as if to highlight just how much taller she was.

"You twerp."

Struggling to think of a more substantial response, I looked away...and she promptly wandered off. This was what made it so hard to keep up with her at times—she was always quick to change tack. Not that I really *needed* to keep up with her in order to hang out with her, of course; I was free to do my own thing.

Then she started swaying her whole body back and forth, so I shot her an inquiring look.

"I'm thinking I might get changed, too. Not sure."

"Huh? Get changed?"

"Into my pajamas, silly. For the sleepover tonight."

"What?"

Who said you were free to sleep here? Because you sure didn't ask ME! I stared blankly back at her. But she ignored me and fetched her bookbag from the desk.

"It's a big house. They won't notice me here. Yep, yep."

She seemed proud of this for some reason. Then she opened her bag and pulled out her clothes and toiletries.

That explains why her bag was looking a little heavier than usual...but you still should've asked me first, damn it!

"You need to warn me when you're planning these things!"

"But if I asked, you'd just say no."

"...It seems you know me well." Spend enough time with someone, and you develop an unspoken understanding, I suppose.

"I know, right?" Nagafuji slid her glasses back on, her expression perfectly serious, like she was trying to look cool.

There's no arguing with this idiot.

As I passed by the mirror, I was horrified to discover that I was grinning like an idiot. Slack-jawed and everything. Hastily, I attempted to press my lips and cheeks back into position.

All because I *briefly* remembered what happened earlier today...

Whew. Good thing Shimamura's not here. If she ever saw me grin like that, I'd probably die.

2. Spring and the moon

I N SUMMER, I always felt lethargic and sleepy. In autumn, I felt chilly and sleepy. In winter, I felt peaceful and sleepy. And in spring, well...it went without saying. In other words, my eyelids were heavy 24/7/365. Pretty wild. Was it my body's way of trying to occupy the time I wasted by not having any hobbies?

Now that I was a second-year, I contemplated adding something new to my schedule. But I was about a year too late to join any clubs, so I figured maybe I could take a leaf out of Adachi's book and get a part-time job. And yet...part of me hesitated.

I didn't have a goal in mind, nor anything I was trying to save up for. And if I wasn't going to have a use for the money, then I wasn't exactly eager to expend my labor.

That said, Adachi didn't seem like the big spender type, either...so why did *she* have a job?

It was right around the time I started to contemplate taking a quick nap that someone called out to me:

"Want to eat lunch together?"

This was the second lunch break of the new school year, and suddenly I was on the receiving end of a social invitation—not from Adachi, but a group of girls gathered nearby.

"You're Shimamura-san, right?" one of them asked.

"Yep, that's me," I nodded offhandedly.

For some reason, every time these new people said my name, it felt like they were referring to Shimamura Co., the clothing company, instead. Was I just paranoid?

"Care to join us?"

The girl in the middle patted the empty seat, and on reflex, I found myself glancing diagonally to the left, at Adachi's desk. Sure enough, she was looking back at me... but then she blinked in surprise and hastily averted her gaze.

"Or do you have plans with someone?" another girl asked with an awkward smile.

"Nope, no plans," I answered, and since I didn't really want to rock the boat, I chose to accept their invitation. "Thanks for having me!" I grinned as I sat down with them. They applauded. *Uh, what?*

Then the three of them introduced themselves. They all spoke really quickly, so I couldn't quite catch their names, but it sounded like Sancho, DeLos, and Panchos... or something like that. Two of them definitely had similar-sounding names. *Way to make this complicated.*

The girl who first called out to me (the one with the glasses) was Sancho; DeLos had a round face; and Panchos had bleached her hair even brighter than mine. This trio had quickly formed at the start of this year, and now I was apparently being invited to join it. Did I look like that kind of social butterfly? Considering they hadn't rejected me outright for slacking on my hair care and letting my dark roots grow out, they clearly didn't care too much about keeping up appearances.

Then I noticed that they all had their bento boxes out, so I rose to my feet. "Actually, I didn't bring a lunch today. I'll go buy something real quick."

Then I looked over at the classroom door...and found Adachi looking at me yet again, her shoulders around her ears, like a timid little dog or cat or whatever. And for some reason, I couldn't bear to turn a blind eye to her.

I knew she wouldn't want to be invited, and wouldn't join us either way, but I walked up to her regardless. Then she flinched and bolted from the classroom with a look on her face like she'd seen a ghost. I was pretty sure the two of us were both headed to the school store to buy a sandwich, and I was going to offer to walk with her, but when I stepped out into the hall, I spotted her running away in the total opposite direction. I knew I couldn't catch up to her, even if I speed-walked. But maybe if I ran…

Conflicted, I briefly glanced back into the classroom—but when I looked back, Adachi was already gone. If I didn't have people waiting on me, I would have been willing to wander around for a bit and search for her, but I couldn't just leave my new lunchmates hanging. Thus, I decided I'd just talk to Adachi whenever she got back to the classroom.

For the time being, my destination was the school store. I didn't encounter Adachi at any point along the way. Then I bought my sandwich. And when I returned to the classroom, I found an empty seat still waiting for me. Then Sancho beckoned to me, so I had no choice but to smile and sit there. I let out a bashful laugh.

"Have you guys known each other long?"

"Not at all. We just met at the start of this year," said Panchos. She glanced at the other two for confirmation, and they nodded.

"Gotcha."

In other words, they probably only invited me since I happened to be nearby. And as soon as there was a seating shuffle, we'd never eat lunch together again. That was probably why I didn't make an effort to learn their actual names.

"Are you in a club or anything, Shimamura-san?" asked Panchos.

"Nope." I shook my head. Then, since it was the polite thing to do, I asked, "What about you?"

"Technically I'm in the garage band club, but I don't attend very often."

"Whoa, you're in a band? Like, with instruments?" I laughed at my own vapid response.

And so the conversation continued.

Honestly, looking back, I'm not sure it was actually all that fun. I remember chewing and sipping and swallowing, but I don't remember what any of it tasted like. Then, right at the very end of lunch, I was finally freed—okay, I take it back. Maybe "freed" isn't a very nice way to put it. Not like I was held there against my will. But to be completely honest, I never asked to join them, so surely I wasn't that obligated to feel grateful about it.

It all happened so quickly. First I changed classes, and then Hino and Nagafuji disappeared, and now I had some new friend-shaped people in my life. They'd probably invite me again tomorrow, and I'd wear my fake smile and pretend to be comfortable. Another day would come and go. *Just a rehash of last year, but with different faces,* I thought to myself as I propped my chin on my elbow.

Then again, Hino and Nagafuji were at least more entertaining, right from day one. But now that we were in different classes, I couldn't imagine myself going out of my way to hang out with them. At this rate, I'd probably end up focusing my energy on new friendships instead.

Looking back over my life, nothing ever seemed to last. Especially not my interpersonal relationships. After I graduated from elementary school, I went on to make new friends in junior high. But those friends didn't follow me to high school, so I had to make friends all over again.

Was this just part of being human? Or was I bad at connecting with people? Was I just a cold-hearted monster?

The way I saw it, I was drifting down the river of fate. And as I spent time in the water, my bonds would eventually become waterlogged and break apart. They just weren't strong enough to stay with me.

On Monday the following week, Adachi stopped showing up to class. While I felt like I knew what had caused it, at the same time, I couldn't fully grasp it. All I knew was that we were barely a week into the new school year and there was already an empty desk in the class-room. It stood out like a sore thumb, and since the seat-ing arrangement was still in alphabetical order, everyone could easily tell who was missing.

It was raining that day, and our previously scheduled track run was hastily changed to a basketball game in the gym. As we were doing our warmup exercises, I gazed up at the second-floor loft. Was Adachi up there? Then again, given the weather, it was possible she hadn't left her house at all. But I had no way to check. Not like I could magically scan for her presence.

If she hadn't decided to skip school today—*okay, maybe I shouldn't assume she's skipping*—if she was here right now, would she be playing basketball with the rest of us? As I caught the ball, I pictured Adachi dribbling. She was a lot better at ping-pong than I was, but when it came to basketball, I was confident I could beat her. After all, I had prior experience, whatever that was worth.

But as I passed the ball back and forth with Sancho, there was no revelatory moment in which I was praised for my "exceptional skill" or anything like that. I tried to throw the ball as perfectly as possible, hoping she would notice, but the ball simply flew back to me, cutting a lazy arc through the air. Maybe all that "experience" had lost its color and started to peel from exposure to the elements.

Every now and then, I snuck a glance up at the loft and debated whether to sneak up there to check for Adachi. Maybe she was waiting for me to come and find her. But if I wasn't careful, I might lead a teacher straight to our hiding place, and it would be such a waste if I inadvertently put it on their radar. So instead I kept looking up there, hoping maybe Adachi would peek her head out.

"Oh, it's Sheema!"

"Sheema!"

Hino and Nagafuji were playing on the other half-court with the rest of their class. They ran past me, Nagafuji playfully pushing Hino by the shoulders, like the world's shortest conga line. But right when I least expected it, they circled back around and ran past me again.

"Hiya, Sheema!"

"Shee-mama!"

"I see you two are the same as ever..."

Especially Nagafuji. I could appreciate the way she simply spoke her mind without thinking too hard about it. If only Adachi could learn to let loose like her, instead of frowning all the time... Then again, I wouldn't want her to be quite *that* ditzy. Maybe there was a happy medium somewhere in between.

"Is Ada-chee out sick today?"

Just because she wasn't standing next to me, they assumed she wasn't at school.

"Probably," I shrugged with a grin. I started to say *we're not conjoined at the hip or anything*, but decided against it. *Didn't someone say that to me a while ago? Where did I hear that?*

"Gotcha, gotcha. Well, see ya!"

"*Hasta la vista*, lady!"

And so the train pulled out of the station, leaving me behind. I giggled to myself.

It felt like we were all being tested on our friendship skills. And while I was passing, Adachi was currently failing. This was...well...a bad thing, probably. The real world was a system built on interpersonal relationships, and as such, not everything was perfectly tailored to suit one's convenience at all times. But while I was capable of accepting that and adapting to it, Adachi honestly wasn't. So where would she go from here? Would she become more flexible, or...?

"That reminds me, Shimamura-san... Are you close with Adachi-san?" asked Sancho out of nowhere. For a moment it felt like she'd read my mind, and I had to struggle not to let the surprise show on my face.

Then, before I knew it, the other members of the Trio jogged over, basketballs in hand. Now I was surrounded on all sides, like a flower with three little petals. This was not comfortable for me.

"Yeah, we're friends, I guess," I shrugged. *Best friends*, according to Adachi. To be fair, I didn't have any particular objections to that label, but...it didn't seem like a smart move to play that card, so I kept it to myself.

"That makes sense. I saw you talking to her a lot last year. Is she sick today?"

So THAT'S why she's asking. For a minute there, I'd thought maybe she saw us holding hands somewhere off campus. And at that point, "friends, I guess" wouldn't really cut it... I chuckled internally.

"I haven't heard from her, but she *did* seem kind of under the weather, last I saw," I told them, since it wouldn't be very cool of me to go around telling other people that she was skipping.

"You know, she and I went to the same junior high, but it feels like she's changed a lot since those days!" said Panchos, the girl on my right. This piqued my interest, and I looked at her.

"Really?"

"Yeah! She still doesn't talk to anyone in class, but she used to be more...uptight?"

She drew her arms in tightly, forming a small mountain shape with her hands. The vibe I got from it was...

stiff. Awkward. In which case, that part of her really hadn't changed at all.

"She's still like that, if you ask me."

"No, really, she was different back then! Like, I didn't sense any *peaceful intelligence*, you know?"

"What does that even *mean*?" Sancho snickered, and in turn, DeLos clapped a hand over her mouth.

At first I was equally confused, but then it started to make sense. If my interpretation was correct, she was trying to say that Adachi had softened up since then. Now *that* would make sense. After all, Adachi was never prickly with me; if anything, she just seemed meek and scared. She didn't bite back—just shrank into herself. Her walls were flimsy, yet deeply rooted.

In the end, I never did check the loft. I couldn't find it in me to swim against the tide, so instead I let it carry me away. Plus, it was nice to play basketball again. *Turns out the "annoying" stuff can actually be kind of fun if you give it a chance,* I thought to myself as I let the ball fly.

After gym class ended, once again, I found myself following the Trio back to the classroom. Something felt wrong, and yet my feet kept moving in time with everyone else's, my lips curling to match theirs, even though I was only half-listening. Coldly, I felt myself transform into a streamlined machine.

We stepped out of the gymnasium, and the wind carried the rain against our backs. It wasn't even all that strong, and yet I could feel the temperature difference spurring me along.

"Spring has sprung, I guess."

When I got home, I sat around and watched my little sister goof off with Yashiro. As loud and annoying as it was, I never got tired of their antics. In fact, it was downright hilarious when you took into account the fact that my sister had only just declared that she "didn't feel like a little kid anymore" at the start of this month when she went up a grade level. Evidently Yashiro brought out her inner child or something.

Then a sharp electronic beep rang out over their gleeful little voices, summoning me. I had dropped my bookbag off on my desk as soon as I got home, and now my phone was ringing from inside it—Adachi, I figured. But when I opened my bag and took out my phone, I turned out to be wrong. I would've thought it'd be one of the Trio, since I just recently exchanged contact info with them, but nope, it wasn't them either.

It was Tarumi.

I hadn't seen her since...what was it, February? And honestly, I was surprised she would call me again. I stepped out into the hall and picked up.

"Hello? Uh...Taru-chan?"

I'd blown the dust off that nickname last time I saw her, so I figured I'd toss it out again and see what happened. *Nope, still awkward.* It didn't really roll off the tongue.

"Hey there, Shima-chan."

Tarumi sounded a little stiff and awkward, too.

Silence.

I was going to ask her, *did you need something?* But then I remembered someone complaining about me always asking that, so I didn't. So what was I supposed to say instead? *What's up?*

Fortunately, I didn't have to think about it for long before she came to my rescue.

"Would you wanna hang out again?"

"Huh?"

On second thought, this wasn't much of a rescue at all. Now what? I already wasn't expecting this phone call, but I *really* wasn't expecting this invitation. Last time around, things were just so awkward...and it hurt. That said, it seemed to recover right at the very end. Was she hoping for more of that?

Don't hold your breath, Taru-chan.

"C'mon, let's hang! Look, uh...I'll try harder this time! You know? Like, I won't...you know...let it turn out like that again."

She seemed to read my mind, because she blurted out a hasty disclaimer. What did she mean by "try harder"? Was she going to talk the whole time, or what? Because that sounded miserable in its own way.

"It's not about 'trying' or...or..."

I was talking to someone who used to be my best friend, and yet somehow I couldn't find the words. I just... didn't see the need for us to go out of our way to hang out with each other. *Doesn't it kind of defeat the purpose if you have to TRY to have fun together?* And yet...it didn't feel right to shoot her down, either...

"Uhhhh...well...okay, sure. Let's hang out or whatever."

"Cool! How about this Saturday?"

"Oh, this weekend?" In other words, we'd potentially be spending a whole day together. "Sure, I don't have any plans."

"Okay. Well then... Ahem..."

"Hmm?"

I heard her clear her throat and figured something important was coming next, so I waited quietly to find out.

"Hooray!"

"...Huh?"

"I'm *soooo* excited! Yaaaay!"

My mind reeled. Was I still talking to the same person? I could hear her breathing stiffen on the other end of the line.

"Or not..."

"Uh...you doing okay there, Taru-chan-san?"

"Th-that was just...an example of how hard I'll be trying!"

Cringe. Reflexively, I took a step back—directly into the wall, where I proceeded to bump my head. *Ouch.*

"Don't you think that's maybe a bit too eager?" *Because I don't know if I can tolerate that for very long,* I thought to myself with a stiff smile.

"Would you prefer something more chill?"

Would I what?

"I guess I'll have to experiment."

And with that, she promptly ended the call. *At least you're decisive about SOMETHING, I guess.* As for me, it felt like a one-sided invasion.

After the call ended, I stood there in the hallway, leaning up against the wall.

My life wasn't exactly *busy,* and yet it felt like all these changes were going to keep me on my toes. And because I was forced to move at someone else's pace, it was running me ragged.

Through the wall behind me, I could hear my sister's innocent laughter. She was always the type to play the good girl whenever she was in public, so it was rare to see her let her guard down around someone who wasn't family. Once upon a time, I was like that, too. And like her, I once had some great friends. But at some point, I ended up *here*. Not that I didn't like my current self, but...I could only pray that my sister would never lose sight of her sincerity the same way I had.

Then my mother peered down the hallway. "What are you doing there?"

"Nothing," I answered.

"If you say so," she replied. "What do you want for dinner tonight?"

"Huh?"

"What kind of food would you want? We're going to go to a restaurant."

And you want ME to decide? In terms of food we couldn't get at home, the options were conveyor belt sushi, Korean barbecue, and regular sushi. Oh, and...

"Okay then, uh..." I paused to think about Adachi. "Chinese."

I didn't choose it because I was craving it—I chose it because I knew we'd end up at the restaurant where Adachi worked part-time.

Sure, I could always call or send an email. But if that was what she wanted, she would've reached out by now. So instead, I'd be better off talking to her in person. Or so I figured, at least.

Sure enough, the whole family ended up at Adachi's Chinese place. Yashiro was no longer with us, though I hadn't noticed her leave.

"I'm looking forward to hearing more about your high school escapades," my mother teased me as we got out of the car. Evidently she hadn't forgotten about Adachi, either.

Somehow I don't think she'll be very talkative this time, I shot back silently.

Then we walked in...and she wasn't there. Instead, a different female employee waddled up to us like a penguin. Apparently Adachi wasn't scheduled to work tonight. Once again, this proved just how little I really knew about her.

"What a shame," my mother muttered offhandedly when she realized Adachi wasn't here.

I turned away...and quietly agreed.

On Saturday, the sky was a single flat shade of blue with a few scant clouds. That day found me standing outside the front gates of my old elementary school. At first I was confused why we wouldn't just meet up outside the train station or something, but Tarumi insisted she was going to handle all the day's planning, so I decided to just shut up and let her call the shots. We were supposed to meet up at 11 AM, but I ended up arriving ahead of schedule, so...now it was time to wait.

As it turned out, it took a lot less time to get here than I remembered. Probably because my legs had gotten *so* much longer. *Heh heh heh.*

For old times' sake, I walked closer to the school building...and when I saw the expanded campus with my own two eyes for the first time, I could scarcely believe it. Obviously I'd heard about it from my little sister, but still, I couldn't help but marvel at how much bigger it had grown. But when I walked around behind the original building, I found the same dirty old walls that were there during my own elementary school days. I could remember running around with Tarumi out here, once upon a time... but the girl in question was still nowhere to be seen.

I checked my phone. *Almost time.* Then I felt my stomach tense up. Admittedly part of me wasn't feeling too optimistic about this... Funny how I never felt this way whenever I hung out with Adachi.

"These things are complicated, I guess."

And with that, I absolved myself of any responsibility to investigate the inner workings of my own heart.

I hadn't heard Adachi's voice in a while now, since she never approached me in the classroom. And now she wasn't showing up to school *at all*, for that matter. What was going on with her?

"Hmmm..."

Whenever I had nothing better to do, oddly enough, I frequently caught myself thinking about Adachi. Partly because I didn't have that many friends to think about, but partly because she was just so *bizarre*. She left a lasting impression, whether she meant to or not. But as I was thinking back to that weird face she had made on the day of our entrance ceremony, I heard Tarumi's voice in the distance: "Crap, you're early!"

I looked up to find her jogging over to me, wearing a light green cardigan over a gray cotton shirt. Yep, pretty normal street clothes. Apparently Adachi was the only person I knew who would show up wearing a China dress. Not that she didn't rock the look, of course.

And so, although the days of randoseru backpacks were long past us, the two of us reunited outside our elementary school.

"What's with the little smirk? Something wrong with my outfit?" Tarumi asked, pulling at her clothes.

Meanwhile, I touched my face. *What smirk?* I couldn't really tell.

"No, nothing's wrong. Sorry, I didn't realize I was smirking."

"Okay, maybe 'smirking' is the wrong word. Kinda seemed like you were...smiling to yourself, I guess?"

"Ohhhh." Now *that* made sense. "I was just remembering this stupid face one of my friends made a while back."

"Gotcha. I'm not late, am I?" She looked up at the round white clock embedded into the front of the school building—the same one I remembered from back in the day.

"No, I was just really early."

"I don't remember you being this punctual, Shima-chan."

"What are you talking about? I've always been punctual!" I laughed dismissively, though it wasn't especially funny.

"Hmmmm... Okay, well, let's do it!"

"Huh?" *Do what?*

Tarumi hunched over like she was charging up for something. I cocked my head.

"WOOHOO! HEY, SHIMA-CHAN!"

"Wh-whoa...!"

The way she shouted and waved at me, you'd think we weren't standing literally right next to each other.

"Alrighty then. Let's get going."

She swiftly regained her composure and turned to leave. Evidently that level of enthusiasm was hard to maintain; she had to charge up for it. Which meant I'd need to stay on guard in case she sprang it on me again later.

And so, off we went. Surprisingly, we were off to a good start. Maybe smiling was more crucial than I thought.

As we walked, I looked at Tarumi. Her hair was still ash brown, and like last time, she was wearing it in loose curls draped around her neck. In the past she used to have straight bangs, but these days her hair was poofy all over.

As our legs carried us away from the elementary school, I breathed a quiet sigh of relief. Given her antics over the phone, I was terrified she was going to propose that we screw around here at our old stomping grounds to "get in touch with our inner child" or something. And as someone with a sibling who currently attended this school, to do so would be a death sentence. If her little friends found out she was related to me, she would never speak to me again.

"Where are we going?" I asked as I followed after her.

"That's for me to know and you to find out," she answered over her shoulder. Then she pointed at my bangs. "So you dyed your hair back?"

I pinched a random strand. "Yep."

"It looks a lot better."

"You think so?"

Not "good," but "better." Everyone in my family said the same thing. The only person who called it "pretty" was my hairdresser.

Then Tarumi reached out—I figured she was going for my hair, but then she touched the hand *holding* said hair. Her fingers interlaced with mine. Then, as my eyes widened in surprise, she turned and started dragging me away.

"Whoa!"

Hastily, I sped forward until we were walking shoulder to shoulder...but even then, she didn't let go. It reminded me of Adachi, except less awkward. In Adachi's case, she was a little too...direct. And another thing—why was it that everyone seemed to want to hold hands with me? Were they trying to keep a leash on me so I wouldn't wander away? This struck me as an absurd misunderstanding. If anything, I was the lazy homebody type.

As we walked, Tarumi glanced over at me. Then she donned a big grin. "How's this?"

In a sense, it was even more intense than the *woohoo* shenanigans.

"Please just say something, would you?"

"Yeah, I was just remembering."

"What?" Her smile held firm, but her brow furrowed in confusion. Evidently her face could multi-task. "I don't understand what that's supposed to mean."

"You used to grin at me like that all the time, remember?" *And I used to not care about what other people thought of me.* I could feel myself smiling slightly as I spoke. "Really takes me back."

Then Tarumi started to look me up and down.

"Hmm?"

"You know, Shima-chan, you've gotten really *adult*... No, that's not it. Ugh, what's the word? God, I'm so stupid." She combed her hair to one side with her fingers as she searched for what she wanted to say. "Basically, what I'm trying to say is, you've really grown up."

"I mean, you've grown more than I have," I replied as she towered over me by half a head. Meanwhile, she maintained her jovial grin—didn't react to the intonation of my voice or anything. Frankly, it was downright unnatural. "You don't have to force yourself, you know."

"Nah, I'm fine," she replied, dismissing my concern with that ever-present smile.

How can she still talk with her lips fixed in that position?

"Besides, I'm only *half*-faking it," she continued.

And with that, she faced forward and started walking a tiny bit faster.

The only sound was that of sizzling. Or maybe "hissing" was more accurate. Either way, it smelled *heavenly*. I leaned forward slightly, gazing down at the *okonomiyaki* pancake frying right before my eyes.

"Hm... hm hm... hm hm hm..."

On the other side of the table sat Tarumi. Her humming sounded painfully forced, and I smiled awkwardly.

It was her idea to come here to this *okonomiyaki* restaurant for lunch. It was one of those places with an iron griddle at every table—in other words, a "cook it yourself" experience. As for the actual cooking part, Tarumi had volunteered to handle it all herself because she claimed to be, and I quote, "really good at it." And as I sat there and quietly waited to be served, sure enough, she seemed quite adept... Whether she was *actually* good at it remained to be seen, but she at least made herself *look* good at it.

Personally, my family hadn't gone out for *okonomiyaki* in god knows how many years, so I was really enjoying the smell and sizzle. My body swayed from side to side in anticipation.

It was the weekend, so naturally, every other table was occupied by families with kids. As far as I could see from where we were seated, we were the only all-girl group in the restaurant. What did girls usually eat instead of *okonomiyaki*? Spaghetti or something? (Yashiro was babbling on and on about spaghetti the other day, so it was fresh in my mind.)

My eyes met Tarumi's, and she immediately flashed those pearly whites again. Granted, it was lovely to be met with a smile purely on reflex, but at the same time...

"You're going to wear your face out doing that."

"No way. This stuff is important...uh...I mean, isn't it?"

She scratched her neck sheepishly. She couldn't even finish her sentence without pausing to question it. But perhaps it was admirable that she didn't let that uncertainty stop her from taking action. And since it would be rude to make her do all the heavy lifting, I decided to make an effort myself.

"So I heard you're a delinquent now. Is that actually true?"

Gripping a spatula in each hand, she looked up from the *okonomiyaki* and met my gaze. "Nah, I just skip school a lot. If anything, I'm a slacker."

"I see... Same as me, then."

To the teachers and everyone else in school, showing up every day was normal. If you didn't rigidly adhere to that, you got slapped with the delinquent label.

"But in your case, you've turned over a new leaf, haven't you?" Tarumi asked as she checked the relative doneness of our pancake.

I shot her a look that said *where did you hear about that?*

"Your mom still calls mine from time to time. That's how I heard about it," she revealed, smoothing her hair as she spoke.

"Hrmmm..."

For one thing, I had no idea they still talked to each other, and for another thing, I *really* didn't want that woman telling everyone my business. I contemplated warning her to knock it off, but knowing the sort of person she was, she'd find my embarrassment hilarious and start running her mouth even *more* to spite me.

Damned if I do, damned if I don't. And for that matter, if you're telling people I "turned over a new leaf," then how about you pack me a lunch, hmm?

"Anyway, they don't talk every single day or anything. And obviously I realize I'm not getting the full picture. So I'd rather hear about it straight from the horse's mouth... Er, not that you're a horse! But yeah, that was kind of my objective today. Okay, maybe not 'objective.' Goal, maybe? Or is that still too aggressive?" She folded her arms in contemplation.

I'd noticed this on the phone with her, too—she had the tendency to hyper-focus on her word choice. As far as I could remember, she had always been the type to shrug off those small details and just have fun.

"Anyway, my point is: tell me about you! Tell me about your school."

Evidently that part of her hadn't changed.

"My school? Uh, let's see..." This time it was my turn to fold my arms in contemplation. Was there anything really worth talking about?

"Are you in any clubs or anything?" she asked.

"Nah. Although for a while I considered trying out for the basketball team."

It was probably a safe move to start with clubs. *But what is "safe," anyway? And what exactly are we starting?*

"Did you play basketball in junior high or something?"

"Yeah. I was usually on the bench, though. What about you, Taru-chan?"

This time, the name "Taru-chan" sounded natural on my tongue. Then again, maybe it didn't count as natural if I was still self-conscious about it.

"Well, I mean, I'm a *delinquent*, right? Wouldn't make

sense if I was dedicating my time to wholesome, school-sanctioned club activities," she snarked.

I giggled. *Oh, so now you admit it?*

"I mean, I didn't start skipping right from day one," Tarumi continued, carefully checking the pancake's color from the side. "Not like I had some kind of truant rep to maintain. And I didn't have a reason to be anywhere else."

"Right."

"But then I started thinking, like, *what am I gonna do with the rest of my life after I graduate?* Completely getting ahead of myself, I know. But the more I thought about it, the more restless I got, until I just couldn't sit around in class anymore. I needed time to think about it. So I started walking around. Observing people around town. It's actually a lot more fun than it sounds."

"Right."

"Like, *oh, I wonder where that middle-aged lady is headed today. I wonder what path she took to get here.* When I start thinking about it, it feels like I'm slowly tracing my way through the town. One person leads to another, and then to another...like dominoes, you know?"

"Right."

"Before I knew it, I got addicted to it...and now I'm a 'delinquent' or whatever." At this point, she seemed to snap back to her senses. She glanced at me awkwardly. "Sorry for rambling."

"No, no, I enjoyed hearing your point of view. I never knew you felt that way."

Plus, it was a lot less work to just sit here and listen.

"Right." Tarumi hung her head sadly, averting her gaze. "You don't know anything about me anymore. And I don't know anything about you."

"Hmm...?"

"Basically, like...I want to know more about you, Shima-chan. And I want you to know more about me."

This conversation was way too serious for a self-proclaimed delinquent like her. But hey, at least she managed to remember to flip the *okonomiyaki*. If it was Adachi, our food would've burned black by now.

"I want to share this moment with you, 'cause like, this moment is all we have, you know?"

Every now and then, I struggled to parse the raw emotion embedded in her words. But there was something about a rough, unpolished surface that really left an impression.

Then she looked up.

"Basically, Shima-chan, what I'm saying is..."

"Yeah?"

"I might be an old friend...er, acquaintance? Whatever. My point is, like...I'm still here, I guess?"

Frustrated, Tarumi combed her hair out of her face. Meanwhile, I was waiting for a translation. Was she trying to say that...old friendships didn't stop being friendships...?

"God, what am I talking about...?" Tarumi muttered, furrowing her brow at her own statement.

"No, it's fine," I replied. "I think I can see what you're getting at."

She waved her spatula dismissively. "Real talk, this is so embarrassing, I think I'd prefer if you didn't."

Honestly, if we started having a heart-to-heart or whatever, I wasn't sure I was going to be able to handle the extreme levels of cringe, so it was probably a smart move to leave some things to the imagination.

"Kssh, kssh, kssh..."

Tarumi started "singing along" with the sizzling, possibly to hide her own shame. As I listened, a dorky chuckle escaped my lips. *Man, I'd really like the food to be ready now.*

Once our okonomiyaki was finished, Tarumi cut me a piece and plated it for me. Then, paying no mind to her own food, she sat and watched me take my first bite.

It was like lava on my tongue, but I didn't want to embarrass myself while she was watching, so I swallowed it and kept a straight face as it burned all the way down. Could she see the tears in my eyes?

"How is it?"

"Oh, um…"

There was an awkward pause in which Tarumi smiled nervously.

"It's really good."

"I know, right?" She smirked at me as she eyed my plate, reminiscent of my mother when she served up her specialty. "You've always liked this kind of thing."

"What kind of thing?"

She pointed at the *okonomiyaki* with her chopsticks. "Remember in Girl Scouts?"

Sure enough, a memory rose to the surface of my mind.

"Oh, right. I remember now."

One time, in Girl Scouts, we all went out for *okonomiyaki* for lunch. I couldn't remember any specific details about it, but…I must've talked about how much I liked it, I guess? And evidently she must have remembered that I liked to add cheese on top, too. *Whoa.*

"I'm impressed you still remember that."

Frankly, I couldn't name a single thing *she* liked. Did that make me a bad person?

"Of course I do. I remember everything about you," she shrugged, scratching her cheek. I felt that first bite of food rise like a lump in my throat—so I hastily went in for another. But instead of eating, Tarumi just watched me.

"Your food's gonna get cold, you know."

"Yeah, I know." But she simply gazed at me, chopsticks in hand.

After we finished eating and had some tea, my stomach was feeling better, so we decided to walk around town for a while. She took my hand like it was the most natural thing in the world, and I didn't stop her; instead, I just let her lead me down Memory Lane. These were the same streets we walked as kids, except now there was a convenience store on the corner, and more intersections, and more grocery stores. But the weathered old signboard with the marble-eyed cat was still there, so that was a relief, at least. *Long time no see, kitty.*

"Oh, hey! There's a store there now!" Tarumi exclaimed and pointed at a sign in the distance. This sign was wooden, and it was all wrinkled, like an old pickle. But the store itself had a rather chic exterior, with a purple and yellow color scheme. There was even a ribbon on the door. But this was perhaps unsurprising, since the sign read *Fancy Goods*.

"Wanna check it out?"

"Huh? Okay."

And so Tarumi led me by the hand into its depths.

Sure enough, the interior was filled with cute little baubles, trinkets, and accessories—in other words, exactly what you'd expect a "fancy goods store" to have. But considering Tarumi had allegedly only just discovered this new store, she sure seemed to know exactly where she was going. She walked straight to the back, to the phone strap section. Then she pointed at the rack.

"Wanna get matching straps?"

"Huh? Okay."

Upon further inspection, these straps were a little too big to hang from a cell phone. Bag straps, I guess. I didn't have any straps on my bookbag at present, so it worked out nicely. But if we were going to get a matching pair, then we'd need to find common ground between her tastes and mine. Perhaps this wouldn't be easy.

"Which do you like?" Tarumi asked, pointing first at a frog, then a cow, then a cat.

"Of those three, I like the cat best."

At one point someone (not sure who) had even likened me to a cat. Probably because I liked to hang out under the *kotatsu* table, I guess. Adachi was definitely more of a dog, though...but what about Tarumi?

"If you wanna get the cat, then let's do that."

She immediately reached for the cat straps, but I cut in hastily: "What about you? We should pick something both of us like."

"I like anything you like." Her eyes wandered around for a moment, then back to me. "I mean, whatever you like is fine," she corrected herself.

Was she was trying to hint that she liked *me*? I could feel myself getting a little bashful. Her gaze carried a heat unlike any other, and it made it hard to breathe. Desperate to get this over with, I reached for the first thing that entered my line of sight.

"Okay then, how about this bear?"

With its oversized head and dopey smile, it was exactly the sort of thing I wouldn't mind attaching to my bookbag.

"Oh, hey, I like that one, too," Tarumi responded. Then, a beat later, she spread her arms out wide, like a ninja clinging to a giant octopus. "I *loooove* it!"

"Do you?"

"Yeah, sure. It's cute enough," she shrugged, and this time she seemed sincere. So I grabbed a second bear off the rack.

Just then, I noticed a man wearing a witch's hat standing next to me, holding the same item. "Man, this little guy is adorable," he grinned. Next to him was a man in a green hat, staring off in a different direction with a disgruntled scowl on his face. Frankly, this didn't really strike me as the type of store a guy could visit with his best bro, but okay. Upon further inspection, I got the feeling I recognized this green hat guy from somewhere... but before I could put my finger on it, Tarumi grabbed me by the hand.

"Quick, let's buy 'em before you change your mind!"

I'm really not that fickle, though... Nevertheless, she dragged me to the register, where we each paid for our own bear. After that, we left the store.

"Now to see if you'll actually put it on your bookbag, am I right?" She grinned like this was some hilarious joke, but I could hear genuine concern in her voice.

"Yeah, of course I'm gonna put it on. What are you worried about?"

"Oh, no, I'm not worried," she replied, shaking her head. But her smile was unnaturally stiff. "Knowing you, you'll probably lose it within a week, huh?"

"Wow! Why are you roasting me like this?" *She makes it sound like I'm some kind of careless bimbo who doesn't take care of my belongings, and...that's not...I mean...!*

"Think about it, Shima-chan. You've never been the type to get too attached to anything," Tarumi replied vaguely, averting her eyes. In a way, it felt like she was making a moral judgment about me...but at the same time, it also felt like she was simply stating facts.

"You really think so?"

"You know what I'm talking about. You're...*unfussy*, or whatever!"

"Oh, right. Yeah...I guess so, yeah," I nodded to myself. Admittedly, that did sound like an apt description of my personality.

As for Tarumi, however...for some reason, she seemed sad. She wouldn't meet my gaze. Oh, but then again, I could see a lot of color in her cheeks. At least her complexion was healthy.

"I'm just worried that...you won't take good care of it."

Now it all clicked. At last, it made sense why she wanted to choose something I liked—because that way, I'd be more inclined to care about it.

"Okay then, I guess I'll have to prove you wrong." I pulled the bear out of its little plastic bag and gazed down at it. It gazed back blankly.

"You mean it?"

"You really don't trust me, huh?"

"Well, you're like a brick wall! You just don't look that serious about it."

I don't? Confused, I ran my fingers over my face, but I couldn't really tell where the problem was.

"But whenever I see you with that blank look on your face, I always wonder to myself...*what is she thinking about?* And at that point, you could say it's both a punishment and a prize..."

At this, her face froze like she'd snapped back to her senses. *Huh?*

"...Or something like that, anyway."

Then she immediately averted her eyes again, like she was embarrassed. But what was so embarrassing about what she said? I tried to think back, but she'd blurted it out so quickly, I couldn't remember half of it. And I got the feeling no amount of ruminating would help me understand the other half.

"Seriously, don't think too hard about it. Just ignore me."

She shook me by the shoulders, but I didn't resist; instead, I let my head bobble around in every direction until it made me sick to my stomach. Admittedly I knew I would be better off just shrugging it off like she was asking me to, since no amount of thinking about it would help me figure it out, but...something else had given me pause. The part where she said she couldn't tell what I was thinking.

I had this one particular bad habit—well, then again, maybe everyone was like this to some extent—*crap, there I go again.* Anyway, I had the tendency to treat my views as the "default," which was probably part of the reason why I never really took an interest in the people around me.

After all, I just assumed they were all the same as me, so what was the point of learning about them?

But for the most part, I was wrong. Most people weren't like me at all. Take Tarumi, for example—we'd spent all that time together, and yet her outlook was nothing like mine. There was a firm line between us, and it felt fresh and interesting to stop and examine it. Once again, if it wasn't for this other person in my life, I never would have realized.

We were best friends in elementary school, estranged in junior high, then reunited in high school. We had followed the same path, and yet we turned out completely different. *Being human sure is wild.*

But would I cross that dividing line to get a closer look at her true self? That was a different story altogether.

After that we wandered around for a while, and I told her the story of when I played with a boomerang at the park, and then I was home again before 3 PM. She walked me all the way there, just like when we were kids.

"Would you wanna do this again sometime?" she asked before we parted ways, her face turned away. Was she feeling bashful, or what?

"Yeah, sure."

Meeting her had opened my eyes to a lot of new things. Besides, she was my friend. What reason did I have to say no?

She whipped her head back in my direction, her bangs fluttering through the air from the momentum. And that same momentum carried her in my direction. *Reminds me of Adachi,* I thought to myself, and before I could finish comparing the two, she took my hand in hers. The way she slid her fingers between mine made my skin tingle.

"Let's be friends again, Shima-chan," she declared, raising our hands up to eye level. And judging from the heat radiating from her palm, I could tell she'd been meaning to say this to me all day.

Real life didn't work like it did in manga, where interpersonal relationships could coast along unspoken in the background. A friendship was like a driver's license—you had to get it renewed every now and then. Not that I knew from experience, obviously.

"Okay."

That was my answer to her passionate proposal. And yet...my gaze flickered to our joined hands. The way this conversation was framed, it felt like she was after something *more* than just friendship...or was I just overthinking things?

She didn't seem to want to let go, and I couldn't shake her off, so instead I just stood there, perplexed. Minutes ticked by. Our palms were starting to sweat like summer had come early, and the weird silence was really freaking me out—

"Oh, it's Shimamura-san," a voice called offhandedly.

Instantly Tarumi straightened up and whipped her hand away, hiding it behind her back. This made me feel like we'd been caught doing something inappropriate, and I stared at the ground. Nevertheless, our intruder barged right in and grinned up at me. It was Yashiro, of course. Probably here to hang out with my sister.

But Tarumi didn't let the introduction of a mysterious child rattle her. It was impressive just how unruffled she was, actually—she didn't even *look* at her. As I stared in surprise, she blurted out a quick "see you" and hurried away. And as she disappeared down the street, I saw the shadow of Adachi in that retreating figure.

The two of them resembled each other—not in their looks, but in their behavior. Perhaps that was why they were both so aggressive in their friendships with me. Whenever I spent time with one or the other, it felt like they were constantly shaking me by the shoulders, jerking me around in all directions.

As I heaved a sigh, Yashiro tilted her head up at me as she clung to my leg. "What's the matter?"

"Oh, nothing. I'm just tired."

Whether it was genuine or forced, Tarumi's enthusiasm

was exhausting to be around for long periods of time. When we were kids, though, I managed to keep up with her just fine... Maybe I was the weirdo in this scenario.

"Who *am* I, really?"

I was on the cusp of falling down the rabbit hole of introspection...but then I caught sight of Yashiro hopping up and down, and her bright blue hair caused other questions to plug that hole right back up again. Was I really that deep of a person? Compared to an enigma like Yashiro, the answer was decidedly *no*. And so I was successfully spared from shallow self-searching.

"Sometimes I really appreciate you, you know that?"

"As well you should!"

I grabbed her by the waist, picked her up, and swung her around. She weighed practically nothing, so it was barely even a workout.

"Are you here to see my sister?"

"I'm here for both of you, of course!"

"Aww, how sweet. Thanks."

This was me: the girl standing here, living, breathing. And with that conclusion, I went on my merry way.

Incidentally, I later received three emails from Tarumi, thanking me for hanging out with her. This, too, was reminiscent of Adachi.

Two weeks into the first semester, the seating arrangement still had yet to be shuffled. Apparently it was scheduled for the end of April.

Keeping with my new routine, I went to the school store, bought my lunch, and ate it with the Trio. I was starting to fit in with them, and as their conversations flew in one ear and out the other, I maintained a smile.

I was a second-year now, and this was my new life. In fact, I was starting to think maybe I'd gotten used to it faster than I thought I would. But then someone else called for me that day at lunch.

"Shimamura."

This was the third unexpected invitation I had received in April, following Sancho and Taru-chan. Third time's the charm, as they say.

I looked in the direction of the voice...and this time, it was actually Adachi.

interlude *Yashiro Comes Calling* PART 6

O N MY WAY HOME from school, I bump into Yachi, same as always.

"From now on, I am Yashiemon, the town mascot," she says to me out of nowhere.

"What are you talking about?"

Other kids from my school turn to look at Yachi as they pass by. Not that I blame them. I mean, just look at her hair! Every time she moves, she scatters sparkles like they're sakura petals. And her butterfly hair matches the spring season perfectly.

"In order to acclimate myself to this planet and this town, I must first establish myself as an idol of the people."

"What?" That's kinda weird. I'm confused.

"After all, I mustn't let anyone discover that I am an alien."

She fixes me with a serious look. That's funny—isn't that one of the first things you said to me when we first met?

"I am not the same as my compatriot, you see. Keh heh heh."

"If you say so. Now be honest: do you *really* not go to school?"

I peer around behind her. No backpack hanging from her shoulders. If she lives in my neighborhood, then you'd think we'd go to the same school, and yet I've never seen her there.

"Are you truant?" Just like my big sister, except not anymore.

"Ha ha ha! Don't be absurd, Little. As I told you, I've long since graduated."

"But you're smaller than me..."

"No, I am not. It is *you* who are small," she declares, standing on her tippy-toes until her legs start to shake. *Hey, that's cheating!* I get up on my tippy-toes, too. Then *my* legs start shaking.

We compete and compete until suddenly Yachi goes "Boing!" and jumps up. Her toes reach my eye level, and... wait, what the? Did I really see that? Confused, I rub my eyes. Meanwhile, she lands back down on the ground.

"It appears I have won."

"Uhhh...okay..." I bob my head up and down as I think back over what just happened. "Did you just jump, like, ridiculously high?"

"I'd say it was average at best. Anyone could do that."

Anyone, huh? Because I don't think *I* could do that. Judging from her looks, she's not from Japan, so maybe her whole country is just really good at jumping.

"Now then, Little, I shall pull anything you desire out of my pocket."

She gestures to her kangaroo pocket, which looks like she sewed it on herself. I peer into it but can't see anything in there.

"Anything?" I ask.

"Anything," she nods.

"Okay then, I want strawberry shortcake," I tell her, since it's the first thing that comes to mind. Then I hold my hands out and wait. Not that I really expect it to work.

"Storeberry shotcake?"

"No, that's not what I said... Whatever. It's a type of cake, okay?"

"Cake?" She tilts her head.

Huh? I tilt mine, too.

"What is cake?"

"You don't know what cake is?"

"Not at all," she declares proudly for some reason.

"A cake is shaped like this, and it's really sweet—well, most of them. My favorite is the normal kind—at least, I think it's the normal kind? The kind with strawberries and buttercream frosting."

As she listens to my explanation, Yachi's eyes shift from left to right. "Hmmm... I'll need to see it for myself first."

"You need an example? Okay, um... Oh, they might have them there." I remember the convenience store that's just up ahead. Pretty sure they sell little cakes there. But first, I need to make sure: "Can you *really* pull one from your pocket?"

"Indeed I can."

She's talking like...like she can make it *out of thin air*.

And so the two of us visit the convenience store on the way home. Honestly, we should probably have a grown-up with us, but Yachi insists she's 680 years old, so we just walk in. Didn't she say a different number last time? I can't remember.

Next to the deli section is a row of baked treats. There's a bunch of different kinds of pudding, but only two kinds of cake: mille crêpe and Mont Blanc. So I take the mille crêpe, since it's the closest in shape to strawberry shortcake, and show it to Yachi.

"This is what a cake looks like. This one doesn't have strawberries, though."

"I see, I see." She takes it and heads for the register.

"You're gonna buy it?"

"Well, I need to find out what it tastes like."

"Do you even have money?" I ask nervously as I follow along behind her. *I sure as heck don't have any money.*

"Money...?" Her eyes wander. "Oh, right. That."

That's not very reassuring, Yachi.

As we walk up to the register, I feel my whole body get stiff. Usually my mom or sister is with me whenever I need to buy something, but this time there's no grown-up to hide behind. *I* have to be the grown-up.

The lady at the register looks like she's my mom's age. She's big and scary. But Yachi acts like she doesn't even notice. "I would like this cake, please," she says, placing the cake in front of the lady.

Then she starts digging in her pocket, and while the lady's staring at her bright blue hair, she pulls out a bear-shaped piggy bank. *What the?!* That thing is *way* too big to possibly fit in her pocket! The cashier lady couldn't see it since the counter was in the way, but *I* sure saw it! It was like a magic trick!

She dumps some 500-yen coins out, one by one.

"How many of these do you need?"

That's a weird question. Can't you see the price sticker right there?

"Just one," the lady replies stiffly.

"Oh, okay." And so Yachi puts the rest of the coins back into her piggy bank...and stuffs it into her pocket like it's the most normal thing ever. *What the heck?!* I scream silently to myself.

But then she walks off without taking her change, so I take the change from the cashier lady in her place. My heart is pounding like crazy. It feels like I'm pretending to be a grown-up, and my face feels tingly.

Then I dash out of the convenience store and find Yachi. She's already opened the little plastic container to get at the cake; she cuts off a small bite with her plastic fork and puts it in her mouth.

I never noticed 'til now, but Yachi's lips are faintly blue. How is that possible? I forget all about giving her her change and stare at her, transfixed. Her eyebrows are really pretty, too. Does she pluck them? What about her hair—does she do anything special to take care of it? How long would it take before it ran out of little blue sparkles?

"This 'cake' is quite good. Very sweet," she declares as she chews. "You should have some, too, Little."

Then she cuts me a bite and holds it up to my mouth. I debate whether to take the fork, but then I notice the cake starting to slip off, so instead I lean forward real quick and take the bite. The fork's pointy ends stab into my tongue slightly, but it doesn't hurt too bad, since it's just plastic.

Sure enough, the cake is super sweet. As I chew, my heart starts fluttering again. Whenever I'm with Yachi, something crazy is guaranteed to happen. She's nuttier than a gag manga. I know I'd never eat cake on my way home if it wasn't for her.

"Would you like another bite?"

"Huh? I mean, it's your cake. You paid for it."

"Go on," she insists, cutting me another bite and holding it up. So I lean forward and let her feed it to me a second time. My sister used to do this for me, too, until I told her to stop treating me like a baby. So why is it okay when it's Yachi?

Again, the taste of sugar fills my mouth. Meanwhile, I stare at her pale, delicate fingers up close. If I licked them, would they taste like cake, too?

Once I pull away, Yachi puts the fork in her own mouth to eat the rest of the bite. Including the part my lips touched. She chews and chews and chews, and then...

"Now that I understand the shape and flavor, I should be all set. Just a moment."

She turns her back to me and starts fumbling around in her pocket. Is this gonna be like the piggy bank moment all over again? I try to sneak a peek.

"Whatcha doing?"

"You mustn't look!" she shouts, like the crane from that one fairytale, and totters away. Then she totters back and thrusts out her hands.

I stare, wide-eyed, at the thing she's holding.

"Here you are," she says, offering it to me.

Sure enough, it's a cake...except she's holding it directly in her hands. One wrong move and the whole thing will fall apart.

"Whoa, what the heck is *that*?!"

"This is the storeberry shotcake you asked for, is it not?"

"Uhhh...not quite..."

I can't believe it. She really pulled a cake out of her pocket! What kind of magic trick is this? Did she secretly buy a second cake? No, that can't be possible. I was standing right there the whole time, and she only bought one! But...the cake she's holding looks picture-perfect...

"Hmmmm..."

I don't get it. Is it a magic trick? Or is the "magic" in Yachi's pocket?

"Heh heh heh. Now you will dedicate all your idolizing to me!" she smirks. I don't think she understands how being an idol actually works.

As I look down at her kangaroo pocket, I frown to myself. All she's done is make herself look suspicious...

But then again, I wouldn't want her to change her mind about giving me this cake, so I guess I'll save my opinion for *after* we eat it.

3. The Moon and Courage

SOME TOOK PITY ON ME, and others were kind enough to ignore me.

This applied to every field trip I ever went on in elementary school. I always wandered around alone, and then when it was time for lunch, I ate my sandwich alone, too. Some teachers would feel sorry for me and offer to accompany me, while other teachers didn't seem to care. And since I had chosen solitude of my own free will, naturally, I preferred the latter. I had no trouble turning down similar offers from my peers, but when it came to authority figures, I couldn't really say no. Thus, I would inevitably end up eating lunch with them, chewing on autopilot until my jaw ached, unable to taste a single thing.

I was fine on my own. I simply didn't care enough about other people to put effort into reading their emotions.

And if I wasn't going to offer the proper amount of respect for others, then I was better off not trying to make any connections at all. After all, I didn't want anyone to get hurt. It was easier to coast through life never causing any problems.

That said, there *was* one time during fifth grade that I purposely went out of my way to try and make friends. I was influenced by all the information bombarding me at the time: *Friends are our greatest assets. Friendship is beautiful. Blah, blah, blah.* So I did my best to smile, and ask questions about the other person, and all that. Then I learned how to spot other kids who were bad at social interactions, and if I targeted them specifically, making friends with them wasn't that hard at all.

But these forced friendships weighed down on me, suppressing my emotions, erasing all my imperfections. Whenever one of them spoke to me, I had to craft a fitting response and keep the conversation going. No part of this was genuine; I just parroted whatever I heard other people saying.

Every time I repeated this process, I grew restless. And every time I gained a new friend, I boxed myself in further, closing off my exits.

But then one day I threw it all in the trash and walked off without them...and that was the day I noticed just how *freeing* it felt. All I needed was a single breath of fresh air to finally realize that I was meant to live my life alone.

There I was, sitting in the second-floor gym loft once again. But unlike last fall, when the place felt like an oven, this time the heat was mild. That, and Shimamura wasn't here.

I sat with my knees tucked up to my chin, gazing out the window, hoping faintly that the spring sun would warm up the icy floor along with the white walls. My body felt like lead, and no matter how much time passed, the weight refused to lift. Even when I closed my eyes, I could still feel it there.

I let out a sigh for the umpteenth time. At this point, I kind of regretted moving up a grade at all. Our lives had changed, and in a blink, Shimamura was surrounded by new people. They walled her off from me, like a protective force field. But I was the only one who saw the wall for what it was; Shimamura *welcomed* the wall.

Long story short: now that we were second-years, Shimamura was thriving, and I...wasn't.

Shimamura wasn't like me—she never hit a dead end in her friendships with other people. Honestly, it was probably sheer coincidence that she came up to the loft back when we were first-years. Something must have pushed her here, and she simply went with it. I had skipped class to be alone, but Shimamura had skipped class out of boredom. Our motives were not the same.

Life was not comprised of neat little chapters; happiness was short-lived and fleeting, lost to the steady passage of time. And the joy I felt at being assigned to the same class as Shimamura was starting to scatter like sakura petals.

I had grown complacent. When she called me by my first name, I knew it was just a joke, but I let it go to my head. I told myself our bond was as strong as an iron chain...and that was when it started to rust.

As I thought back to the way Shimamura had acted in class, I hung my head until my forehead touched my knees. She had smiled at those people—a polite and vaguely friendly smile, probably reserved for anyone she didn't know well. I knew that, but the problem was...I couldn't tell the difference between that one and the one she always directed at *me*.

I was so irrationally frustrated, both at Shimamura *and* the girls she smiled at, that it made me want to claw my own face off. I felt so petty for feeling betrayed over this. My heart ached with despair, and I wanted to cry.

I really thought we built something together...but whatever I had with Shimamura, it wasn't special or magical. It couldn't support our weight at all. Instead, it fell apart faster than a sandcastle.

And yet, in choosing to come here of all places, I was clearly hoping Shimamura would prove me wrong.

I sat up a little taller, then hunched back down, as I debated whether to sneak a peek down at the first floor. Eventually, when I decided to take a quick look, I spotted Shimamura down there. Apparently they'd decided to hold gym class indoors today, probably because of the rain. I could hear basketballs thudding against the floor. Was Shimamura throwing a ball around right about now? Did she notice I wasn't in class this morning? Was she thinking about me? Did she suspect that maybe I was up here?

I thought about spying on her, but if by any chance she looked up and caught me, I wouldn't know what to do. So instead I played it safe and waited. I could hear the rain drilling against the wall behind me.

Then I heard footsteps, and I looked up. Someone was coming up the stairs to the loft. I couldn't stop myself from smiling like an idiot as I watched to see who it was. For some reason, I wasn't remotely scared that it was a teacher coming to lecture me, either. My heart was filled with light.

But as I would quickly discover, that light would sting my eyes.

It wasn't Shimamura. It was some girl I didn't recognize. When she noticed me sitting here, she reacted awkwardly, but otherwise kept walking right on past me to the corner. Then she sat down, legs extended and crossed, and took out a small paperback book. Her hair was a long, dark, indistinct mass, concealing her elongated, oval-shaped face. I quickly lost interest and let out a sigh.

Once again, I had lost my place.

If I can't be with Shimamura, then I'd rather be alone—that was my entire motivation for coming here. Disappointed, I decided to make my retreat. So I grabbed my bookbag, slung it over my shoulder, and headed down the stairs.

As I contemplated where to go next, I heard footsteps from above.

"Uh, wait! You there!"

The other girl had followed after me to the landing. Clinging to the handrail, she bent forward to look down at me. I fixed her with a wordless, inquiring look. She smiled.

"Sorry I stole your spot."

"...It's fine."

I tried my best not to be rude, in case she was an older student. So I inclined my head slightly and hurried out of the gym before anyone in my class could spot me... and before I had to look at Shimamura having fun with people who weren't me.

Outside the gym, there were no teachers—just the faint patter of rain. As I tried my best to stay dry, I found myself steadily moving away from the school building. Then I felt the weight of my bookbag against my shoulder and decided it was too much effort to turn back...so I didn't.

Not like I'd left anything behind.

As I biked along down the street, I gazed around at the scenery and wondered to myself: *Where am I going?*

I left campus on autopilot in the exact opposite direction of my house. Belatedly, I realized I didn't want to risk encountering my mom back at home, since she'd probably chew me out. But biking around town didn't exactly make the time fly by; I was fully conscious of every agonizing second that passed. The vague warmth of spring mixed with the rain to create a state of torpor that slowly engulfed me.

I passed by the driving school and cut through the parking lot of the men's clothing store until I arrived at the same shopping mall I'd visited with Shimamura a handful of times in the past. I didn't have anywhere else to be, so perhaps this would suit my purposes just fine. I parked my bike and hurried inside, out of the rain.

The interior had been remodeled at some point last year to add new stores. As I walked along, the scent in the air shifted to something sweet. Someone once told me about how malls in other countries all smell the exact same way. Then, as I passed by the electronics store, I picked up the scent of maple syrup.

If Shimamura was here with me, which stores would she want to visit? I contemplated this question as I walked. We didn't have any plans to come here together, and yet I couldn't help but think about it anyway. Honestly, I still didn't have a firm grasp of her likes and dislikes. How could I get her to enjoy herself with wild abandon? She had zero hobbies—she literally said as much to my face—so it was kind of impossible. Not like there was a boomerang store here.

I wanted to know *everything* about Shimamura...well, unless she secretly hated me or something, in which case I didn't want to know about it. But if I *did* know about it, then maybe I could figure out a way to change her mind, so maybe I *did* want to know about it. So yeah, I wanted to know everything about Shimamura. *Everything*.

But now we were second-years, and I'd scarcely heard her voice at all. Well, okay, technically I'd heard it a lot. But it was in the background, not directed at me. Sure, I could just call her up on my cell phone, but that wasn't the issue. *So what do I actually DO about this? What is it that I want to change?*

I wanted...to be with Shimamura. I wanted to hear her voice. I wanted her attention. That was the honest truth of how I felt, and I wasn't trying to turn a blind eye to it. But there was one thing I could say for sure: I wasn't going to fix anything by wandering around the mall on a weekday afternoon. So what was I doing here?

There were twenty-four miserable hours in a day, and I hadn't spent a single one of them doing anything productive. I could sum up the entire day's events in a single breath. How did each day manage to be both long and short at the same time?

It felt like I was living in monochrome. Everything was so dull without Shimamura. *God, I'm such a boring person.*

As I walked along the far edge of the mall, I picked up the sounds of chatter—animal chatter, to be specific. I glanced around and swiftly spotted what appeared to be a brand-new pet shop with not only puppies and kittens, but fish and...even sheep? At least, according to the sign outside.

"This could work."

Maybe there was a chance Shimamura would take an interest in this kind of store.

As I examined it further, I noticed another teenage girl standing out front, scanning the store, almost like she, too, was scoping the place out. Toying with one of her long, loose curls, she peered in through the open door. She was a bit taller than me, and she radiated an aura of maturity that suggested she was older than me, too. Then she sensed me staring, glanced at me, and moved to walk away—but she was apparently so startled, she slammed her bookbag right into mine.

"Sorry!"

The impact knocked something loose, and it fell to the floor. I caught sight of it, stopped short, and bent down to pick it up. It was a little bear strap. But its owner didn't seem to notice that she'd dropped it; she was still walking. Conflicted, I debated what to do about it, but ultimately decided it'd be a real jerk move to let her walk off without her bear...so I gave chase.

"Hey, um, wait," I called timidly after her.

She turned back, her bangs fluttering with the motion.

"You dropped this." I held out the bear strap.

She took it and looked down at it. "Oh, thanks." Then she did a double-take. "*Oh!* Oh my god! Thank you so much!"

Apparently it meant a lot to her, in which case I was glad I plucked up the courage to get it back to its owner. But if she was at the mall on a weekday afternoon, then she was probably a delinquent... Not that *I* had any right to judge her, obviously.

"I must've been fidgeting with it too much... Ugh, I need to be more careful... Seriously..."

And so she walked off, petting the bear. She was actually friendlier than I was expecting based on her looks. *I guess she must really love that little thing.* I was never interested in bag straps, so I didn't have any, but... maybe if me and Shimamura had matching ones...

"That sounds nice..."

Specifically the part where no one else was involved. That part was crucial. Mandatory, even. Very important. Because other people *loved* to butt in on my time with Shimamura.

Since I was already standing in front of the pet store, I decided to have a look inside. The entrance I chose apparently led to the back of the store, because the first thing I encountered was the aquarium section. The air in here was uncomfortably humid; I scanned around, then moved on to the next room, where I found...the insect and reptile section. I decided to give it a passing glance and move on.

The next room was narrower, and by far the most deafening—the bird section. A parrot beat its wings against the confines of its cramped cage, using its beak to struggle valiantly with the door lock. It was so aggressive, I was half-afraid it might actually get it open. The next few minutes were spent watching with bated breath; then I slipped out of the bird section to the front of the store.

Here, puppies and kittens were relegated to their own separate glass cases, with separate beds for each of them to sleep in, surrounded on all sides by uncomfortably pristine white walls. Surely this was no way for an animal to live.

Then, as I passed by, one of the puppies woke up and rushed over to me. Startled, I recoiled slightly. Standing on its hind legs with its front paws propped up against the glass, it wagged its tail at me, tongue lolling. Almost like it was trained to do this to tug at my heartstrings... and it was *working*. I could feel tears start to prick at the corners of my eyes.

I felt no sadness looking at the birds in their cages or the fish in their tanks, and yet these glass cases provoked an emotional response from me. Why? As I gazed down at the little white puppy, I realized: because it felt like looking in a mirror.

I, too, was a puppy on display. Even worse, I'd basically put myself in the glass case on purpose. But instead of trying to act cute, I just sat there.

Now that I was faced with a perfect mirror image of myself, it shook me to my core. The root of my sadness was self-pity.

"...Never mind. This place sucks."

And so I decided against bringing Shimamura here. Wiping at my damp eyes before the tears could fall, I hurried away from the metaphorical mirror in the direction of the nearest exit.

Once I made it outside, my plan was to walk around the perimeter to the bike parking area. But as I walked, I spotted some sort of attraction set up against the wall near a different mall entrance.

A woman was seated at a long table decorated with a banner that read: *Get Advice For Love, Money, Marriage, and More!* She looked to be in her late twenties, though her face was concealed behind a purple veil. Classic "mysterious fortune-teller" aesthetic. Her skin was as pale as plaster, throwing her crimson cheeks into sharp relief. But with her visible lack of makeup, she struck me as somewhat unsophisticated. Her setup was first-rate, but she seemed like a total amateur.

"Welcome, welcome! Have a seat," she called, gesturing to the chair in front of her, even though we hadn't so much as made eye contact. I tried to pretend she wasn't talking to me, but before I could walk by, she continued, "You can go ahead and take your worries home with you, but your tomorrow will be just as ugly as today."

Reflexively, I stopped short.

Then I heard her pat the table. "Come, come."

I turned back to look at the fortune-teller(?), unsmiling. In contrast to her singsong voice, her expression was dead serious.

"Hurry on over, now," she pressed, beckoning to me.

The banner shifted slightly. My eyes settled on the first half: *Get Advice For Love*. Not that my "worries" were all that *love-related*. Well, not really. I was pretty sure it was something else. But the more I thought about it, the more I risked setting my cheeks ablaze in public, so I timidly walked over.

Admittedly, part of me was concerned that this was a scam. But the fact of the matter was, I was in a vulnerable state of mind.

Before I sat down, I took another look at the fortune-teller. Her expression remained gravely serious. At the very least, she seemed more trustworthy than the headbanger swinging her hair around on that one horoscope TV show.

"Are you a real fortune-teller?" I asked, comparing the person in front of me with her somewhat professional setup.

"Yes, I suppose so. A fortune-shaman, if you will."

"...Okay..."

I'd never heard of that job title in my life, and it kinda sounded like she just invented it. Also, upon further inspection, her crystal ball had a crack in it.

"I can divine anything. For example...let's see...I can tell you where those tears came from," she declared, pointing at my eyes.

I straightened up sharply.

At this, she grabbed her crystal ball, set it in her palm, and gazed at me through it. "Yes, I see it... You're lovesick."

Again, I flinched, shrinking into myself slightly. This, I believe, was my downfall.

"You're so easy to read. What a sucker—I mean, what a sweetheart! Ahem!"

She started fake-coughing, but I was too flustered to care. She hadn't even looked at my palm yet...so how could she tell? Er, not that I was *lovesick for Shimamura* or anything. That would just be weird.

"Heh." With a tiny chuckle, the fortune-shaman gently held out her hand, palm up. "One thousand yen."

"What?"

"Normally this would cost at least three thousand, but you teenagers are too cheap—I mean—I'll offer you a student discount."

Her expression was firm, and yet her lips were loose enough to make wildly unnecessary comments.

"I have to pay a thousand yen for this?"

"Frankly, you're getting a real bargain."

She held out her hand once more. But the word "bargain" only made me *more* suspicious. Not that I expected her to do her job for free or anything, but I innately questioned the value of anything priced above 500 yen. Maybe it was just human nature.

That said, I was already sitting here, and I got the feeling this lady wasn't about to just let me walk away. Her fingers wiggled impatiently. So I took out my wallet, and as I pulled out a one thousand yen bill, my brain calculated the cost equivalent at my workplace: two lunch specials. As I placed the bill into her palm, she snatched it up like a vacuum and tucked it away into her pocket.

"Thank you."

Evidently she took better care of her money than she did her equipment. This was not very reassuring.

First the horoscope show, and now this. Am I just drawn to this stuff? I really need to make sure I don't get duped into wasting my money. But at the same time, it felt like it was probably too late.

After that, the fortune-shaman seemed to grow tired of holding up the crystal ball, so she set it back down and scrutinized me directly. I could practically *feel* her gaze sliding over every inch of my body...over my uniform... All at once, I was overcome with deep regret. I wanted nothing more than to get out of here and go home. So I decided I would count to five, and if she was still ogling me, I would grab my bag and run.

But the fortune-shaman seemed to read my mind. "I do have one question about this person: is their hair longer than yours?"

"What person?"

"Your beloved."

The word *beloved* made me think of Shimamura, and *that* made me blush furiously.

Be-love-d. Love. This was the kind of thing I could never say aloud, but at the very least, it felt more accurate than trying to say I was *in love* with her.

So, which of us had longer hair? Honestly, I had never thought to directly compare my hair to Shimamura's. I thought back to all my most recent memories of her.

Usually I was looking at her from the side rather than the front, which was depressing. From what I could recall, she hadn't given me even a passing glance these days. And of the times she *did* look at me, she usually had an awkward smile on her face...

"Oh ho. That bad, hmm?"

"...What?"

Once again, I hadn't said a word, and yet she was already smirking.

"If you can't even answer that question, then I already have all the information I need."

"...You do?"

I couldn't believe it. *Oh god, what if she read my mind?* One minute all the blood had drained from my face, and the next minute I was blushing all over again.

"I see what it is you lack. And what you lack is *courage,*" she declared in the midst of my panic. "It's as plain as the nose on your face! You're hiding because you're afraid of what others will think."

She was completely right. I stared back, stunned. Was it really that obvious at a glance? At this point, I was genuinely concerned that this woman might be able to read minds. She was a fortune-teller, after all.

But for as impressive as it was, something felt off.

"I shall teach you an easy way to gain the courage you need. Go stand over there and start shouting."

"*What*?!"

She was pointing at the mall interior, at a passageway just a few feet away. Granted, it wasn't the most populated area, but we weren't exactly alone out here, either. I could easily imagine the sorts of weird looks I would get if I started screaming for no reason.

Dubiously, I looked back at the fortune-shaman, but she simply picked up her crystal ball and smiled calmly. "You can choose not to, of course, if that's your preference. All you'll lose is the thousand yen you paid."

Now I deeply regretted paying up front.

"If you want to get your money's worth, then get out there."

I flinched, and my chair creaked. Again, it was as if she had read my mind.

Every now and then, I thought back to this one time in junior high when I worked as a library assistant. There was this girl—I couldn't remember her name or even what she looked like, but she asked me if I had any friends. At the time, I told her I didn't, and that I was fine with it...but looking back, I couldn't help but wonder why she asked me that. Was she going to offer to be my friend?

Even then, my answer would have remained the same. I would have told her I didn't need any friends. But part of me regretted how that interaction played out. Part of me felt that we should have talked it out first, like actual human beings, instead of me one-sidedly slamming her with rejection.

With that in mind, I didn't want to add to my list of regrets. I couldn't keep sticking my head in the sand. No, I was going to take action. And if I ended up regretting *that*, then so be it.

As I rose to my feet, my sight went black, as though I'd closed my eyes.

"Raise your fists and make your declaration. It's the only way to carve it deep into your heart."

As I started to raise my arms, it occurred to me that this lady seemed less like a fortune-teller and more like a life coach.

"I...I can do this," I said aloud in a barely audible whisper as I glanced around at the people nearby.

Meanwhile, the fortune-shaman sat at her table and critiqued my attempt, her chin resting in her palm. "Your voice is too quiet, your statement is too vague, and you're not raising your fists. What's the matter?"

If I—

"If you had that kind of courage, you wouldn't need advice, is that it?"

My arms flinched as she read my mind.

"Heh." Another tiny chuckle. "Think about it in reverse: with enough courage, you can solve any problem. Now then, let's see you try again."

Her words swayed me. At her insistence, I straightened up. "I'm gonna...do my best!"

"This is your best? I don't think so. Try again."

"Oh, come on! Uhhh..."

I raised my arms, then retracted them again. I couldn't think of anything else to shout, so I looked to the fortune-shaman for help.

"No backing down," she cautioned me.

No backing down. No running.

"...I won't back down from this."

"What was that?"

I...I...I won't...

I won't...back...down...

Three, two, one—

"I WON'T BACK DOWN!"

The next thing I knew, my arms were in the air. My mind went blank. My vision went white. Beside me, I could hear applause.

"Oh, that's wonderful! One more time."

"I! WON'T! BACK! DOWN!" I yelled at the top of my lungs.

My eyes felt like they were bursting. Something shot up from the soles of my feet all the way to my skull, and by the time my ears stopped ringing, all that remained was an almost drunken lightheadedness. I staggered back to my chair and took a seat.

"Wonderful," the fortune-shaman repeated, chin in hand. "I didn't think you'd actually do it."

"Thanks, I guess...?"

"People don't need to *know* the future. They only need to *want* it."

The way she spoke, it felt like she'd dropped the fortune-teller pretense in order to level with me. For once, her words struck me as sincere. "I, um..."

But just then, her gaze shifted to the right. "Oh dear, dear, dear."

I retracted what I was about to say and instead followed suit.

Someone was running in our direction...someone wearing a navy-blue uniform... Belatedly, I realized it was a mall cop. My eyes flew open, and the blood drained from my face. Why was a mall cop barreling towards us?!

"Looks like we made too much noise."

The fortune-shaman clucked her tongue in annoyance. Without wasting a single moment, she yanked up her banner and used it to wrap up everything on her desk in a single bundle. Then she leapt to her feet, knocking her chair over. She was moving so quickly, my brain couldn't keep up.

Yet again, she let out a tiny chuckle. "Well then, I'll be going now. May your future be bright." And with that, she slung her bundle over her shoulder and took off running like a real class act. Something told me this was how her crystal ball got cracked.

The mall cop ignored me and went after the fortune-shaman. Part of me was relieved, but the panic was still there. Was she some kind of unlicensed fraud fortune-teller? If so, I was apparently a *terrible* judge of character.

Then again, being unlicensed didn't necessarily make you a fraud, did it? Maybe it was just bureaucracy keeping her down. Sure, she took one look at my uniform and assumed I'd run away from school, and the rest of her observations were shallow at best, but in the end, her advice was the real deal.

Something had quietly taken root inside me, convincing me that the thousand yen I paid was worth it. All I could do now was take a deep breath and wait for it to bloom.

The next day at school, I spent the morning hiding up in the gym loft. Quietly, I exhaled. Without any hobbies of my own, I was an empty void, filled halfway with thoughts of Shimamura. Without her, what would I have left? I would probably just sit around and stare into space, like I was doing right now.

Down on the first floor, I could hear lots of voices. Apparently the first-years were having gym class; I could feel the vibrations from their footsteps through the floor, and it almost felt like the sounds filled the room all the way up to the roof.

Dazedly, I bobbed my head up and down. This was a big, fat waste of my time. The seed planted in me yesterday was still smoldering weakly.

But as I craned my neck around, suddenly, I spotted something lying on a dusty ping-pong table—something that wasn't there last time. And by this point, I was bored enough that this tiny change drew my interest.

Carefully, to avoid being seen, I crawled over to the table. Resting directly on one corner of the table was a small paperback book with a bookmark sticking out of it. Was this the same one that girl from yesterday was reading? It was placed too perfectly to have been carelessly forgotten... Maybe it was her way of saying "this space is reserved."

Casually, I picked up the book and looked at it. It was missing its dust jacket, but the title and author were still listed on the front cover. Apparently it was written by someone named Kitsukawa Eiji; I wasn't a bookworm, so I didn't know who that was.

I flipped to the page where the bookmark was placed and started reading. Obviously I wasn't expecting anything to make sense, since I was starting partway through, but one passage in particular drew my attention:

"Why did I keep running away, you ask? The answer was simple: because I was afraid. Day in and day out, I was terrified to think that my future was going to leave me behind. So, rather than let things change without me, I chose to take the initiative myself."

It was a rather abstract piece of writing, and I didn't fully grasp what it was getting at. Not that I was expecting this single passage to single-handedly explain the main character's motivations, of course. That said, the words "leave me behind" rendered me dizzy. I read the passage again and again and again. Then I put the book back where I found it and sat down on the spot.

I stared up at the lights on the ceiling as though I was gazing up at the soul leaving my body. This random nobody author had somehow picked the exact combination of words necessary to ignite the seed inside me.

Shimamura and I both shared the same classroom, but only she was functioning as a second-year. Meanwhile, I was stuck in the past.

My mind reeled. My *body* reeled. It felt like my eyes were rolling around in their sockets, and it frightened me. Times like these, thinking about Shimamura was the only thing that helped me keep it together...on the outside, anyway. On the inside, my heart was a total mess.

In the end, it was safe to say that Shimamura was my entire life. She was the basis for all my decisions. So, seeing as Shimamura was on my mind, what was my next move?

Then the bell rang to signal the end of class and the start of lunch break. Girls would flock to Shimamura, and she would sit in the classroom and eat her lunch.

I pinched my bicep, willing myself to stop holding out hope. *She won't come up here. You know that. You know for a fact that she won't, so give up already.* I could feel my jaw slacken from zoning out, so I pursed my lips tightly together as I pushed my daydreams away.

How long was I going to waste my time entertaining this delusion that if I sulked for long enough, Shimamura would come check on me? Something spurred me forward, warning me that I needed to act before it was too late.

Too late for what?

This thought dragged up the fear buried deep inside me. What if Shimamura and I actually stopped being friends because of this? What if our friendship died because I sat around up here for no reason?

I stared, wide-eyed, unblinking. Lukewarm tears filled my vision as my eyes attempted to lubricate themselves. There was no emotion behind them; if I wiped them away, no more would take their place. These tears operated independent of sadness.

There's still time, something whispered.

But what could I do? Could I join the group of other second-years gathered around Shimamura? Objectively speaking, it would probably make everything really awkward, if I was being completely honest with myself. But while I understood that...there was still a tiny chance that I could fit in with them. Maybe that option was available to me, and I just hadn't noticed.

But if I took that route, I would stop being myself.

I wasn't perfect; I couldn't predict the future. I knew that. So what kind of person was I? What was I afraid of losing?

Right now, I was empty, but stable. In spite of the nerve-wracking impatience I felt, deep down, part of me was comfortable—content with being alone. When it

came down to it, I was naturally disposed to solitude...
but that didn't mean it was what I wanted.

In a sense, "making an attempt" was always the correct
choice over the alternative, but this way of thinking had the
tendency to forego actual personal growth. After all, you
could justify any meager effort as "an attempt" and simply
give up afterwards, leading to a slow decline. If I wanted to
better myself, then I needed to do the impossible.

I rose to my feet and started walking. I could feel my
back threatening to hunch over, so I stood up straight
and faced forward.

Honestly, it was stupid of me to expect anything of
other people. Well, okay, maybe that was an exaggeration.
But there was no point in making other people solve my
problems for me—it was *my* responsibility. Other people
couldn't feel my emotions; only I could locate the pain.
Thus, it was up to *me* to do something about it.

Without any hobbies of my own, I was an empty void,
filled halfway with thoughts of Shimamura. Without her,
this was all I would have left...so the solution was simple.

As I hurried down the stairs, I thought back to yesterday.

"I can do it, I can do it, I can do it..."

My heart trembled as I gave myself a running start.
Then I threw my arms into the air and shouted the magic
words:

"I WON'T BACK DOWN!"

And then I immediately bolted from the gym. Apparently the fortune-teller had rubbed off on me in more ways than one.

I went to the school store, bought whatever looked appetizing, and headed to the classroom. There she was, surrounded with people, smiling faintly, looking at someone who wasn't me, just like any other day. Each of these things served as a strong deterrent. There was no space for me there.

But as it turned out, I could always just make my own.

This time, I didn't let the presence of other people stop me from calling out to her.

"Shimamura."

And that was the moment I truly became a second-year.

"**A**KIRA, can we talk?"

We had set up Hino's shogi board and were in the middle of a game when her mom walked in. I hadn't seen Hino's mom since Bring Your Parents to School Day back in sixth grade, but she was wearing a fancy kimono at the time, so I recognized her right away. Well, okay...I recognized the kimono. Her face, not so much.

"Oh, hello there, erm...Tae-chan, was it?" she asked tentatively. But although she didn't sound too confident, she was more or less correct, since "Tae-chan" was what Hino called me when we were little. I considered telling her my actual name was Taeko, but instead I just nodded.

"Yep, that's me."

"Yes, of course," Mrs. Hino nodded in kind. Then she immediately turned back to her daughter.

127

Clutching my lance piece in her hand, Hino donned her "I'm annoyed with you" scowl and glanced over her shoulder. "What do you want?"

"Perfect, you're already dressed. I'd like you to say a few words to our guests, please."

"What? Why should I have to talk to them?"

"Because you're a member of this family."

"*Great.* Fine, I'll be right there. Gimme a minute." She set her captured piece down, then turned to me. "We gotta put the game on pause. But I'll be right back as soon as I get it over with."

"Huh? Okay." I nodded firmly.

She pressed a finger against my forehead. "*Behave yourself.*"

"Of course I will! I'm an expert at that."

"You liar. You've got 'troublemaker' written all over your boobies."

She reached out to grab my chest, so I karate-chopped her hand away and smirked. *Nice try.* These days I had a preternatural sense for when she was about to do it.

With a stiff smile, she rose to her feet...but by the time she took her first step, that smile was gone. "This is why I try to stay out as late as I can. To *avoid* this crap," she muttered. And with that, she and her mother left the room.

Now I was alone.

First things first...I looked down at the shogi board and stole a few things I was confident Hino wouldn't notice were missing.

"Now then..."

I glanced around Hino's room, but I'd already combed through it to my heart's content, so there was nothing left to entertain me. I crouched down and scanned the manga on her bookshelf, but even then, nothing grabbed me; I'd already borrowed every one of these from her at some point in the past. The rest of the bookshelf was filled with books about fishing, and I had *zero* interest in those. How long was she going to waste her time fishing when the rest of the world had moved on to boomerang throwing? *Get with the times.*

I stepped away from the bookshelf and wandered aimlessly around the room for a while until I completely ran out of things to hold my interest. Hino still wasn't back...so I decided to step out into the courtyard for a while.

"I just have to 'behave myself' while I walk, that's all."

But how would I go about achieving that? The best compromise I could think of would be to keep my upper body as still as possible while I moved.

Sounds complicated, but I guess I can give it a try.

With my posture perfectly straight, I stepped out into the hall. Already the pressure on my shoulders was more intense than I had anticipated.

Yeah, I'm gonna regret this in the morning.

As I gazed out at the sunlit courtyard, a breeze blew by, rustling the branches of the trees. Today's weather: sunny, yet windy. Beyond the tall surrounding fence, beyond the fast-moving clouds, I could see patches of bright blue sky.

I took a deep breath, then exhaled. Hino's house felt like a samurai estate, or a ryokan, or a summer home—quiet and peaceful, like we were out in the middle of nowhere. It felt like I was on vacation somewhere far away, and to me, it was a lot of fun.

I wanted to walk out into the yard, but then I remembered I was in my socks. I thought about it for a little while, then decided to take 'em off. Problem solved.

I stepped down onto the gravel. If this was summertime, the rocks would burn the soles of my feet, and if it was wintertime, they'd feel like ice cubes. Fortunately for me, it was springtime, so instead it felt like a nice foot massage.

Idly, I wondered what Hino was up to right about now. Was she kneeling formally in front of some bigwig? I was tempted to sneak a peek, but I knew it wouldn't be easy. After all, Hino was *really* good at catching me.

"...Hmm?"

Right as I was making a flute out of a leaf I found, a small girl walked out from inside the house. She was wearing some kind of kimono, so at first I thought maybe it was Hino. I squinted through my glasses. *Nope, not her.*

It was a little girl, even younger than Hino by the looks of it, wearing a scarlet yukata with a green *obi*. Pinned in her long black hair was an ornament with a bell; under her arm, she carried a yellow helmet, like the kind you'd see at a construction site. Was she on a walk, too? Her behavior was really inconsistent; one minute she was peering into the courtyard pond, and the next minute she was playing with the cobblestones at her feet. *Oh, now she's coming this way!*

Despite her short legs and *zori* sandals, she was pretty speedy. She slid right up to me.

"Aha. Here's a big girl."

She smirked up at me. Like with Hino, I could sense *you-know-what* about to happen, so I swiftly recoiled. Sure enough, her little hand closed on empty air mere inches from my chest. That was how I knew I'd made the right call.

"Oh ho. Not bad."

The girl retracted her hand, then looked me up and down. I didn't enjoy being ogled, but I was supposed to be *behaving myself*, so I couldn't really protest too much.

"You don't appear to be a child of this family."

"No, I am the child of a butcher."

I swayed my body in a suitably humble manner. She swayed back. So far, she seemed like an alright kid... except she talked down to me like she was older than me, and for some reason I just went with it.

"The butcher's daughter, eh? Does that mean you can eat all the meat you want?"

"It's hard to say."

She tilted her head sadly. "Sounds like a no, then."

Thinking back, the first time I spent the night at Hino's house, it was because I'd eaten some of our products without permission. My parents had launched into this giant lecture, and I wasn't about to stick around for that. Back then, Hino was *excited* to have me over.

"Hmm? Why are you barefoot?" the girl asked, staring at my feet.

"Well, my shoes are by the front door," I explained, lifting a foot and spreading my toes. "And I was wearing socks earlier, but I didn't want to get them dirty. See?"

I had tucked them into the hem of my skirt for safekeeping, so I pulled one out. After all, I didn't want her to think I was some kind of uncivilized barbarian. But for some reason, the little girl tilted her head back and let loose a roaring laugh. "Every place has its weirdos, I guess!"

Why does everyone think I'm weird? Even Hino calls me weird. What did I ever do wrong?

"Now then, I've had my fill of tea and snacks, and I'm getting bored, so I think it's time I hit the road."

She actually ate that crap? None of the snacks they served here were remotely sweet, so I didn't care for them. Did they serve her the good stuff or what? Who even *was* she?

"Earthlings are so fascinating. Some hate being big, and others hate being small."

Cackling, she turned to leave. The way she spoke, she made it sound as if she was an alien or something. *And you're calling ME the weirdo here?* She donned her yellow safety helmet, hopped onto the moped parked out back, and drove off.

On second thought, if she has a driver's license, then maybe she IS older than me.

"I guess you can't judge a book by its cover."

Take Hino, for example. Despite her small size, she was actually pretty mature.

After that, I went back to playing with my leaf flute. Unfortunately, no amount of practice made it sound like a real flute.

"What the...? What are you doing out here?"

Just then, Hino spotted me and came barreling towards

me nearly as fast as the other girl. When she reached me, I scooped her up in my arms. She started to flail.

"Hey! Put me down!"

"Okay."

Back on the ground, she put a hand on her hip and glared at me. "Listen here, you little twerp!"

"What's up?"

"I told you to *behave yourself*, dang it!"

"I did. It gave me a neck cramp."

Now that she was back, I decided it was finally safe for me to relax my shoulders. *Agh, my neck.* I turned my head from side to side, stretching it. Meanwhile, Hino let out a sigh...but thankfully, by the time she looked up, she was smiling again. This was a welcome sight.

"Are you done talking to your guests?" I asked.

"Well, one of them ran off somewhere, so I lied and said I would 'go look for her.' Now let's go back to my room!"

Glancing nervously over her shoulder, she pushed me down the hall. Was she referring to that girl in the red kimono? If so, she really did me a solid by giving Hino back to me so quickly.

When we stepped back into Hino's room, she scanned around. "I see you haven't been up to any mischief in here."

"Of course not! How rude!"

"I can never be too sure with you. That's all I'm saying."

As she spoke, she went back to her side of the shogi board. Then she looked down at it...and her expression hardened. "Uh, hello? Care to explain this mass exodus?"

"It's a wage strike."

"You're telling me my *king* went on wage strike?"

"Wait, what?" Maybe I took one too many.

"...Fine, whatever. Let's just keep playing and see what happens."

Instead of putting the pieces back the way they were, Hino gave up and decided to resume the game.

You're going to have to put in a lot more effort than that if you want to beat me, I smirked to myself as I moved a piece. Then she moved a piece. Then I... *Uh oh, I'm stuck. I think the game got harder somehow.*

"I notice your mom hasn't come after you," I commented.

"Mmm... My family doesn't expect much of me. And I mean that in a good way."

"I see." *Well, okay then. Anyway.* "I'm looking forward to lounging in your giant bathtub later tonight."

"Good to know."

"You could even join me! Yeah, let's take a bath together!"

"Wha?!"

The silver general slipped out of her hand. I tried to catch it but missed.

The bathtub at my house would be way too cramped, but here at Hino's house, we could both fit—just like old times.

"See? Your house is the best," I told her.

"How old are we again...?" she muttered as she picked up her general. Then she scratched her head. "Let me guess. This is the real reason you came over, isn't it?"

"Correct."

That's my Hino. She knows me well.

Likewise, I knew she would burst out laughing.

4. Courage and Friendship

HOW LONG HAD IT BEEN since I last heard Adachi's voice? This was quite possibly the first time she'd spoken aloud in the classroom since we moved up a grade.

At the sound of my name, I looked up to find her standing next to me, her nose and lips looking tense and rigid. As usual, she moved like a rusty robot in need of grease, to the point that I wondered whether her joints creaked. Just looking at her made me uncomfortable.

So you WERE at school today. I'll bet you were in the loft, like I suspected.

Next to me, the Trio all stopped eating and stared up in confusion at the intruder.

"Can I sit next to you?" she asked me.

I didn't mind, of course, but what about the others?

I looked around at them. They looked back at me blankly, their eyes wandering timidly. No one spoke. Then again, the question was posed to me, so perhaps it was my call to make.

"Go for it," I answered.

That said, we didn't exactly have an empty chair ready for her. As I craned my neck, scanning the room for one I could borrow, Adachi knelt down beside me. Problem solved, I guess. Then she set a to-go bag from the school store on my desk with a loud *thud* that caught my attention.

"Isn't that kind of a lot?"

She had three...no, *four* different sandwiches? *Who are you, Yashiro? You sure you can eat all that?*

"You can have some if you want."

She opened the bag to show me its contents. Granted, I already had a sandwich of my own, but hey—*free food is free food, right?* So I figured I'd take a look. Honestly, it was a pretty generous gesture, coming from the same girl who used to make me buy her lunch for her all the time. Of the items inside, the jam bun appealed to me the most, but...I hesitated to take it.

"Hmmm..."

I stared down at my stomach. Obviously I couldn't exactly pinch it in front of everyone... That said, I knew for a fact that Adachi wasn't going to be able to eat all this on her own. Thus, I ultimately decided to help myself to the jam bun.

"If you want a second one, go for it."

"No, that's okay. I can't eat three. Thanks, though."

At this, her expression finally softened, and her lips curled in a faint smile. The tip of her nose was red, possibly from all the effort it took to hold her face in that position.

Once she started unwrapping a sandwich, the rest of us took that as our cue to go back to our food. But while all of us kept looking at Adachi, she only ever looked at me. She didn't acknowledge the Trio at all, as if they didn't exist to her. Uncomfortable with her presence, the three of them ate their food in total silence.

She was a meteor that had broken through our tepid, laid-back atmosphere, tearing a hole in the ozone layer, letting all the air escape. And I couldn't think of a single way to patch things up again.

Meanwhile, she sat at my feet like a guard dog. Looking at her made me restless. *Are there really no empty chairs?* I glanced around again, and this time I spotted one, so I rose to my feet and walked over. Then, with permission from the other people nearby, I dragged it back over and offered it to Adachi.

"Oh, thanks."

She got up and sat down on it. Satisfied with my solution, I returned to my seat.

But, as it turned out, this fixed nothing. Her focus was still entirely on me, to the point that I could practically *feel* her gaze. Our eyes met; she looked up at me with her usual puppy-dog eyes as she took tiny, unenthusiastic bites of her sandwich. With her eyes so full of emotion, she was utterly unlike her robotic classroom persona, and it felt like she was probing me for something... I gazed back, trying to figure her out.

I could sense the Trio giving us weird looks, but it didn't bother me much. Honestly, maybe it was for the best that Adachi came back before I managed to get too emotionally invested.

The silence lingered. And it would continue to do so unless Adachi took a different stance. But I knew she wouldn't, and so nothing would change. She had zero intention of fitting in with everyone; as far as I could tell, she literally didn't care about anything except being with me. She came back to the classroom with the express purpose of sitting here.

While part of me had reservations about this "no one else matters" attitude of hers, another part of me shrugged it off as just Adachi being Adachi. Nothing she did fazed me anymore. And while I didn't know exactly what influenced her to come back, I understood what kind of person she was, and therefore I understood that it must have taken her a great deal of courage and will-power. This was probably why my reaction to her was so different compared to the Trio's.

Out went the warm spring air, and in came chilly tension. Couldn't she feel their pointed stares? Didn't it bother her? Honestly, if I'd been in her shoes, I would have kept my distance. Not to say that she made the wrong choice. *To each their own,* I thought to myself, knowing full well it was a convenient shield for my own cowardice.

For some people, it was impossible to have too many friends; for others, one was enough. Everyone had their own individual needs, and...well...at the risk of sounding totally full of myself, Adachi seemed to have decided that I was the only one she needed. But if that was what made her happy, then there was nothing wrong with that.

As for me, I sometimes wondered whether I needed any friends at all. And I had yet to find my answer. All I knew for sure was that the hole in the ozone would come at a price...and at this rate, my friendship with the Trio most likely wouldn't even hold out until the next seating shuffle.

After school, Adachi sped over to my desk like it was lunchtime all over again. Maybe she wanted to make sure she was the first person to get there this time.

"Let's, uh, walk home together!"

I looked up at her wordlessly. After a beat, she blinked and furrowed her brow anxiously, which made me laugh.

"Sure," I grinned. At this, Adachi realized I was being a bully.

"Were you being mean on purpose?" she asked, pouting slightly.

"Nahhhh, of course not!"

Dismissing her concern, I grabbed my bookbag and rose from my chair. I could feel someone looking at us, but I decided not to find out who it was. Not like that knowledge would really change anything.

That said, we couldn't really "walk home together" when we lived in two different directions. We'd only get as far as the front gates before we'd be forced to part ways. Of course, there was that one time on the day of the opening ceremony where she came with me all the way to my house, then walked home from there, but I was pretty sure she wouldn't make that same mistake again anytime soon. Hopefully.

As we left the classroom, I gazed at her face in profile. Sure enough, her gaze was flickering to and fro, just as I'd anticipated. For some reason her eyes were always damp and emotional, like the protagonist of some vintage shoujo manga. Then we headed down the stairs, and she caught sight of the bear strap hanging from my bag. Her eyes moved back and forth in time with its movements.

Since she seemed so captivated by it, I held it up for her to see.

"Is... Is that bear trendy right now?" she mumbled awkwardly.

"I don't know about trendy, but he's definitely popular," I replied.

As far as I was aware, he was one of those classic cartoon characters everybody knew about, on par with Anpanman. At the very least, they were literally hanging on the same rack at that one store. And considering those two guys were looking to buy one, he clearly appealed to a wide demographic.

"Pretty cute, don't you think?"

I'd promised Tarumi I would take good care of the little guy, and I liked to think I'd kept my word thus far. Incidentally, my little sister must've been really envious, because she took one look at him and immediately made plans with Yashiro to get matching straps of their own. At one point Yashiro said, "I didn't realize such a creature inhabited this planet." *Ha, I wish.*

"Where did you buy it?"

"You want to get one?"

"Uh, y-yeah...I wouldn't mind having a bag strap, I guess."

"Interesting." *Honestly, it's not that hard to find a store that sells bag straps,* I thought to myself. But maybe Adachi really liked this particular character.

"Th-then we...we could...match... Ha ha heh..." A clumsy laugh left her lips. Kinda like an airplane that failed to achieve liftoff.

So THAT'S what she wants, huh? I didn't see the appeal of it myself, but oh well. Classic Adachi. Oh, but if she bought the same bear as Tarumi and I, wouldn't that make the three of us a matching trio?

Okay, maybe not.

Once we left the school building, I figured I'd walk with her to the bike parking area...but then she reached out and took my index finger in hers. Hanging her head, she looked up at me.

"Can... can we hold hands?"

As she spoke, she clenched her hand into a fist around my finger, and at that point, my answer didn't really matter.

"Sure, go for it," I shrugged, and a split second later, she engulfed my entire hand. Whereas Tarumi had consistently gone for my left hand, Adachi always went for my right.

Come to think of it, Adachi didn't know about Tarumi at all. No surprise there, since their paths never crossed. But if they ever did...somehow I had a feeling that things would get *complicated*. After all, Adachi didn't really seem like the type who was good at sharing her toys.

As we held hands, she used her free hand to unlock her bike and pull it out of the rack. From my perspective, it seemed a lot more efficient to hold hands *after* she retrieved her bike, but she had different priorities, apparently. She dragged both me and her bike all the way to the front gates.

This was as far as we could go together.

"See you later, Adachi."

"Right."

As we said our goodbyes, she looked at me longingly.

"Oh, come on. We'll see each other again tomorrow, won't we?"

"Yeah."

"You're coming to school, right?"

"Yeah..."

She muttered something else under her breath; I couldn't quite catch it, but I thought I heard my name somewhere in there. Something about coming to see me?

If I was her whole reason for going to school, well...that'd be flattering.

Anyway.

"Uh, hello? Earth to Adachi-san?"

"Huh?"

"I kinda need you to let go now? So I can go home?"

I raised our joined hands to eye level. After all, I couldn't exactly pull myself free when she had the added weight of a bicycle on her side.

"Oh, right!"

Hastily, she moved to let go of me...then stopped short. Her cheeks and nose flushed pink as the corner of her lips twitched.

"I...I won't let you go."

"What?"

She blushed even redder, and her lower lip started to quiver. *Uh, you okay there?*

"I won't let you go!"

"Yes, you said that."

"Go...go...go..." She wilted rapidly.

Evidently she was trying to make a joke and it fell spectacularly flat. She stared at the ground with a look that I remember previously referring to as her "pathetic puppy-dog look." Her hair drooped down her shoulders like dog ears.

Not to be a total jerk or anything, but...this was a lot funnier than her actual joke.

As I stood there grinning at her, she looked up, blushing. "Uh...c-come with me real quick."

"Huh?"

She started to drag me away, and sure enough, I didn't stand a chance against her added weight. As she led me in the opposite direction of my house, I found myself passively hoping we weren't going too far, but otherwise didn't protest. Thankfully, however, she came to a stop just around the corner from the school—out back, across the street from the farm fields.

Then I remembered: Adachi was technically a delinquent. *Maybe she's about to show her true colors and steal my lunch money,* I joked to myself. But then she stepped right up to me—

"Wh-whoa."

—and wrapped her arms around me in a hug. One arm around my back, one around my neck. She pressed her slender frame against mine.

"I... You see, I...!"

Don't shout in my ear! It was so sudden and loud, I reflexively recoiled.

"I...I like you..."

It was just like Adachi to start off at full volume only

to immediately peter out. Apparently she liked me, but didn't say how much or in what way, so I wasn't really sure if I should be flattered or overjoyed or what. There was no further explanation; all she did was squirm nervously against me.

Her face was buried against my shoulder, and I could feel its heat. If I waited a few minutes, would smoke pour out of her ears? The girl was so flammable, she was practically made of straw. *Maybe it's safe to start asking questions now.*

"So, uh, why did you...hug me all of a sudden?"

I started to say "pounce on me," but it felt a little too critical in my head, so I went with something else. I couldn't see her expression, but I could feel her breath against my neck.

"Because...it's been forever since..."

"Since we hung out?"

"Since *anything*. You're always with those...those other girls."

I felt her fingers dig into my back. At the surface level, her answer didn't make sense, and yet...amid the forlorn sadness, there was a tiny barb mixed in. And once it fully wedged itself into my ear, it all clicked.

"Ohhhh." I patted her lightly on the back as vague understanding settled in. "So basically, you were jealous?"

Her neck stiffened, and that was all the answer I needed. I shook my head and smiled.

"You hopeless dork," I sighed, my breath gently ruffling the hair near her ear. Then I reached out and smoothed the strands back into place.

Evidently Adachi saw me not as a big sister, but as a mom. Thinking back to the one encounter I had with Mrs. Adachi, it made sense why her daughter might look for that kind of affection elsewhere. That said, it was a lot to ask of a fellow teenager.

Smiling stiffly, I averted my gaze. If the Trio or someone else from our class were to see us right now, they'd totally think something else was happening, and there'd be all kinds of rumors flying by tomorrow morning. It was hard to say whether Adachi ever took those sorts of concerns into consideration, though. Maybe she simply didn't care.

As I pondered this, I continued to rub her back. Then, once it felt like enough time had passed, I asked, "Are you better now?"

Slowly, Adachi pulled away—so gradually, it almost looked like she was floating away in a zero-gravity zone. Her face was so flushed, you'd think it was wintertime all over again. Like we'd gone back in time.

But that's just Adachi for you.

Here on the soil of our second year, we had built for ourselves a flimsy straw house. Now it had burned to the ground, leaving only an empty meadow...and Adachi was the one who struck the match.

"Alright, kiddo, it's time for everybody to go home! That includes you, Sakura-chan!" I told her, patting her head.

"Why are you talking to me like I'm five?" she protested, looking up at me, her ears pink.

I think you'll find the answer if you pause to reflect on the way you've been acting.

"I'm gonna need you to let go of my hand now, okay?"

Shoulders shaking and eyes narrowed, she slowly let go. We were both so slick with sweat, I half-expected our hands to pull apart like half-dried glue. I gazed down at my now empty palm. I could still feel her warmth... *What are we doing?*

"Okay then, can I...call you later?" Adachi asked, as if in exchange for my freedom. Evidently she still needed more attention.

"Sure, I don't mind."

Although I had to wonder if there was really anything worth talking about. Would we just sit there in silence, like always? Awkward phone calls were already hard enough for me as it was. Add in Adachi as the other participant, and the onus would fall on *me* to keep the conversation going. That was what I hated more than anything. Maybe someday I would have enough social graces to be able to simply enjoy the silence, but today was not that day.

Still, my response had made Adachi smile...and maybe that was all that mattered.

"Okay, I'll call you at like...seven-ish, so...yeah." With that, she leapt onto her bike and sped off down the street like a madwoman.

Seven?

"But that's dinnertime..."

Guess she can't hear me, I thought to myself with a shrug. So I gave up on trying to reschedule and decided to head home. As I walked, I smoothed my uniform back into place and scratched my itchy neck.

I had kind of assumed most people ate dinner somewhere between 6 and 7 PM, but evidently Adachi's household operated differently. Admittedly, I couldn't really picture her eating dinner at a set time each day.

She and I were the same age, but our different childhood environments—the homes we grew up in, the people who raised us, the things we experienced, the things that stayed with us—had made us into two very different people. And I found that sort of thing really interesting.

"Can we have dinner early tonight? I'm starving," I lied to my mother, so I wouldn't have to go to the effort of explaining to her the real reason.

"I beg your pardon?" Annoyed, she turned back to look at me. "I'm making it right now," she shot back flatly. *Yeah, I know, but that doesn't answer my question.*

"Would you like some egg bolo cookies?" Yashiro asked, offering me the whole bag. Lately it felt like she'd become something of a regular here at the Shimamura house... Nevertheless, I took one, and was relieved to find that they still tasted the same way they used to when I was a kid.

"How about I serve you first?" my mother asked me. Evidently she hadn't ignored her daughter's request after all.

"Yes, please," I answered, and took a seat at the dinner table. Something told me my little sister was going to throw a fit about it later, but oh well. "What are we having?"

"Store-bought roast chicken."

If it's already cooked, then what are you hacking it up for, lady?

"I'm looking forward to it," the little blue gremlin announced as she sat down next to me. I looked at her dubiously, and in response, she...held up the cookie bag again. "Want another bolo?"

No thank you.

And so I ate my dinner ahead of the others, then returned to my room. Knowing Adachi, I figured she might lose patience and call me a good thirty minutes early, but then 6:30 rolled around and there was still no sign of her. So I switched on the TV, set my phone down next to me, and waited.

Thinking about it, I'd dedicated basically the entire second half of my day to Adachi. The dam had burst, and her feelings had rushed out in a mighty torrent that swept me off my feet. Not only that, but it had washed away the past two weeks of lead-up into the new semester at school. Starting tomorrow, I anticipated that my daily routine would look completely different... *Yeah, it's gonna get busy.*

Was Adachi sitting by the phone, counting down the minutes until 7 PM? I could picture her sitting cross-legged on her bed, hunched forward, peering down at her phone. I adopted a similar position; *yep, this feels about right.*

Then my sister came in to complain about me eating dinner without her, and Yashiro came in to deliver me more bolos, and before I knew it, my phone rang at exactly 7:00 on the dot. Her timing was so accurate, she was like a human cuckoo clock. I switched off the TV and answered the phone.

"...Shimamura?"

She didn't even bother to say hello first. *Why would you need to make sure it's me? You're the one who called!*

"It's me, alright! Good evening!"

"Oh, uh...g-good evening..."

"Are your legs going numb?"

"Huh?! Wait, what? How did you know?!"

I'll take that as a yes. I burst out laughing. And as I laughed, Adachi's panic intensified. I could hear her moving on the other end of the line, like she was glancing around... What, did she think I installed some hidden cameras in her room or something?

"Just thought I'd ask. So anyway, what's up?"

"What do you mean, what's up?"

"I thought you wanted to talk about something," I pressed, though my hopes weren't too high.

"Uhh...not really."

Knew it.

"It's just been a long time since we talked on the phone, that's all."

She made it sound as though we used to have regular phone conversations, but that couldn't be further from the truth. We had no interests or club activities in common, so what were we supposed to talk about? We didn't even have any independent hobbies—*nothing*. Honestly, it was a miracle that a pair of oddballs like us had managed to stay friends for six whole months now.

"Don't you want to have friends, Adachi?" I asked, thinking back to earlier at lunch. Once again, I ended up in charge of picking the topic.

"Huh? Uh...not really. I'm not super interested," she replied curtly. Talking to her on the phone always seemed to bring out her more introverted side. It was hard to believe this was the same girl who would aggressively hug me or try to hold my hand.

"I mean, I..." she began, tripping over her own words. Then she fell silent.

"You what?" I asked, helping her up.

"I have you, so...yeah."

What does THAT have to do with anything?

It took me a minute to realize that this was her excuse for not needing friends.

Honestly, this wasn't quite the answer I was expecting to get. I had anticipated something more along the lines of "*You're* my friend, Shimamura." And sure, she had essentially said the same thing using different words, but... man, Adachi was subverting my expectations like crazy today. *Looks like I might be in it for the long haul with this one,* I thought, and adjusted my sitting position. Using my folded futon as a cushion, I stretched my legs out.

"Do you talk on the phone with other people, too?" Adachi asked suddenly. Or maybe it wasn't really that sudden, but it certainly felt that way. I just didn't really get why she was asking.

"Sure, sometimes," I replied, thinking of Tarumi. *If she's Taru-chan, and I'm Shima-chan, what would that make Adachi? "Ada-chan"? Nah, that'd be weird.*

"You do?"

Her voice was as hard as diamonds. Either she was actively upset about this, or she was simply matter-of-factly confirming my statement. Zero enthusiasm.

"Is that a bad thing?"

"Well, I was kinda hoping it was just a you-and-me thing...since I don't talk to anyone but you..."

"What was that? I couldn't hear you."

I could, actually, but it didn't really feel like I was supposed to. *If you want to mutter to yourself, then save it for after the call, please.*

"...It's nothing."

Didn't really seem like nothing, but okay. I didn't really want to press her on it, so I decided to drop the subject. "If you say so."

"Yeah."

Once again, the conversation died. I checked the time. Not even five minutes had passed. Bored, I rubbed my big toes together and contemplated what to do. Adachi was the last person to ask a question, so maybe it was my turn... Yeah, that seemed about right. Not sure why I felt so honor-bound to "take my turn," but at the very least, it seemed like a fair solution.

To skirt around the awkward tension, I decided to offer my belated gratitude:

"Oh, right. Thanks for the jam bun, by the way."

"Oh... Sure, no problem."

Should've known better than to expect a conversation out of that, I thought to myself with a wry grin. But believe it or not, Adachi actually did have a follow-up.

"So you like sweets?"

This was such a normal question, it actually caught me off guard. I thought back over our days in the gym loft. Had the topic never come up before? Apparently not. Back then we weren't trying to build anything with each other; all we did was exist.

"Yeah, I love sweets. Is there anyone in the world who doesn't?"

Granted, I didn't love them quite as much as my kid sister. Seriously, if you saw how much she ate, you'd think she was the Princess of Candyland.

"Then...would you want to go out for sweets sometime...?"

"Huh? Sure."

Donuts? Soufflés? Maybe crêpes this time?

"Okay, uh...c-cool."

If she was trying to sound excited, she failed completely. Her voice was so stiff, I could picture her shoulders hunched up around her ears.

Once again, we had descended into the valley of silence, and it was getting to be a real hassle hauling both of us out each and every time. Or maybe I was just out of shape, so to speak.

"Alright, well, should we hang up now?"

"What?!" Her voice was so panicked, I could practically hear a dramatic echo behind it.

"I mean, we're running up your phone bill just sitting here."

"Oh, don't worry. I've got plenty of money for it."

"Isn't it kind of a waste to spend money on *silence*?"

Especially since she earned that money by running around in a China dress. It was the kind of thing a girl like me could never wear; only a pretty girl like Adachi could make it work. But I digress.

"Not at all! I mean, if you think about it, uh...this way I get to..."

"Get to what?"

I heard a restless tapping sound on the other end of the line, like a sugar addict waiting on their next fix. Then the sound stopped, and there was a pause...and then...

"As long as I have you on the phone, I...get to have you all to myself...so yeah," she finished clumsily.

For a minute, I was rendered speechless. It was just so... *intense*. But looking back over the course of our friendship thus far, it wasn't really a surprise.

"You know, Adachi..."

"...Yeah?"

"You can be pretty possessive sometimes, you know that?"

Considering what went down at lunch, she *really* seemed like a little kid who couldn't share her toys.

"Uhh...I mean, just a normal amount, I'd say..."

"That's a bit of an understatement, if you ask me!"

"No, really! I'm... I'm completely normal!"

Judging from the way she repeated the word "normal" over and over, it sounded like she was fairly flustered. I could picture her eyes darting nervously in all directions... and the mental image spurred me to continue.

"Oh, just relax. It's nice to know you love me, regardless of how you choose to express it."

As soon as the words left my mouth, the embarrassment kicked in, and I started laughing to play it off.

Oh god, what if she can tell that I'm embarrassed? Kill me now!

I listened with bated breath, trying to gauge her reaction...but I couldn't hear anything. Usually I could at least hear her breathing on the other end, but this time there was actual genuine *silence*. I checked my phone; the call was still connected. Confused, I froze.

Then, out of nowhere, Adachi started gasping and coughing, like she'd come up for air after holding her breath. (For her sake, I won't describe the exact sounds she was making.) Anyway, once she collected herself, I could tell she was going through some kind of teary-eyed self-loathing, so I spent a good chunk of time cheering her up, or smoothing things over, or whatever you want to call it. But at least it gave us something to talk about, so in a way, I kind of...appreciated it, I guess?

Once the call started to wind down, I checked the time to find that approximately thirty minutes had passed. Granted, most of it was silence, but still, it was one of the most successful phone calls I'd ever had.

"Well, I'll see you tomorrow at school. Don't skip, okay?"

"You..."

"I what?" *Why is it that she can never finish her sentences?*

"You...you better not skip either...so there!"

Her weird mid-sentence pauses made me laugh. For some reason, she and Tarumi both kept defaulting to some cheerful persona with me, and it never really worked out for either of them.

Wait...does that make it MY fault?

After that, Adachi seemed reluctant to actually hang up, so I counted down from three and hit the End Call button.

Whenever we were together, I always ended up having to take charge, and honestly, it was exhausting. I just wasn't the leader type... Now that the call was over, I drew my knees up and hugged them to my chest.

"Nnnngh..."

A low groan escaped my throat. Was tomorrow going to be like this, too? Or did Adachi get it all out of her system today? Maybe she'd be a little more relaxed by tomorrow. But then again...relaxed or not, I was pretty sure she'd still make a repeat attempt. She'd approach me, and everyone else would withdraw, creating an isolated bubble with just me and her.

Being with Adachi limited my possibilities. After all, the fewer people in my life, the fewer opportunities I would have. As I examined this fact without weighing its relative pros and cons, I thought to myself: *well, obviously I should choose what's best for me.*

Adachi had committed herself to a path without other people. Well, okay—maybe "committed herself" was a bit of an exaggeration. For a teenager, though, it was a pretty significant move.

"But the path I choose is..."

I slowly closed my eyes, hoping someday I'd find the words to finish that sentence.

"**M**NNN..."

It occurs to me that I'm basically just pretending to do my homework.

I glance over at Yachi. She's watching TV with my big sister, sitting between her legs and leaning up against her. Now my sister's got blue sparkles all over her neck and chin. But she doesn't notice, 'cuz she's starting to fall asleep. She's always so sleepy in the springtime. I wish she'd at least change out of her uniform when she gets home from school. Meanwhile, Yachi's grinning and eating her egg bolo cookies.

Looking at them all cuddled up together, I can't focus on my homework at all. But which one am I mad at? There's this fuzzy feeling in my tummy, and it won't go away.

"Hmm?"

Neechan catches me looking at her and glances over at me, her gaze unfocused. Our eyes meet, and for some reason I start feeling kinda awkward.

"Are we being too loud? Want me to mute it?" she asks, putting a hand on Yachi's head as if *she's* the problem. But Yachi keeps grinning.

"You should join us, Little."

For some reason, her innocent invitation makes me super mad. "Wh... No way! I don't... I don't even want to! And I've got homework, anyway!"

"What a good little student."

"Good on you!"

They start praising me, but I know they don't actually care. Frustrated, I scratch my head. Then I go back to my homework, do one or two more problems...and stop again. Secretly, I shoot another glance in their direction. Once again, Neechan is nodding off while Yachi grins.

"Mmnnnn..."

Invite me again, dang it! Silently, I curse my stubbornness. And some other stuff.

"Hey, uh, Yachi? Come here for a sec," I called, since I knew for a fact that Nee-chan was too lazy to get up.

"Yeeees?" Yachi answers, slowly turning in my direction.

"I think I need help with my homework."

I don't *actually* need help, but Yachi doesn't question

me for a second. Instead, she smirks. "Keh heh heh! You've come to the right place."

Then she runs right over to me. On one hand, it's a relief...but on the other hand, I kinda feel like a jerk for lying. The two feelings swirl inside me like a storm.

"After all, I am the great Yashiemon."

You're still talking about that? Really?

Behind her, Neechan sprawls out on the floor, limbs splayed in every direction.

"So, what's this?" she asks, peering at the textbook lying open on my desk.

"Uh...math...?"

I thought it'd be obvious, considering all the pluses and minuses and stuff, but the look on Yachi's face suggests she honestly has no idea. She's clueless about a *lot* of stuff... Reminds me of the cake incident from the other day. How can she claim to have graduated school when she doesn't even know what math is?

"Hmmm..."

"..."

"Ah..."

"..."

I sit in silence and wait for her to finish mulling over whatever it is she's thinking about. She keeps murmuring and looking at the textbook.

Then, suddenly, she slams it shut, looks at me, and says, "&##$%."

"What?"

"I repeat: &##$%."

...I really can't understand what she's saying, so I mimic the sound back to her. "Oraaha?"

"Yes, precisely." She nods, satisfied, her arms folded smugly.

"What language is that?"

"Alienese."

"Alienese?!"

"It is some kind of slang from before I was born. I don't know what it means."

What happened to *yes, precisely?!*

"Would you like me to tell you about outer space?"

"Uhhhh..."

"Where shall I start? You see, my tribe has an average lifespan of approximately 800 million years, which is comparatively longer than most others..."

Gleefully, she launches into a tangent. I can't tell whether she's telling the truth or making it all up. For that matter, I never said I wanted to hear all this, but now I'm stuck listening to it. She keeps tossing out these *giant* numbers, the likes of which you'd never, ever see in a math textbook, and it feels like I'm totally trapped.

But my sister doesn't come to save me. Instead, she rolls over onto her side and keeps on sleeping.

Meanwhile, I shoot a glance at my textbook.

Don't tell Yachi, but...I'm starting to think she can't do math.

What if Shimamura was a cat?

   "Shimeow..."

   What if *I* was a cat?

   "Shimeow!"

   ...Not sure why, but something tells me we'd both have the same meow.

5. Friendship and Love

FOR ALL INTENTS AND PURPOSES, I was a fairly normal person.

Sure, I had a few quirks to my personality. But overall, I had nothing special going for me. No magic powers, no sixth sense; I could only interact with what was directly in front of me. And my biggest fear was that Shimamura might change into someone I didn't recognize while I wasn't paying attention. The thought terrified me, so I decided the solution was to keep my eye on her as much as possible.

And that's exactly what I did.

"Um...Adachi?" Shimamura called, smiling awkwardly.

I turned and looked at her—and accidentally bumped her shoulder. *Oops.* Maybe I was sitting a little too close.

She glanced around for a moment, then exhaled. "Never mind."

Shimamura was always quick to shrug off a lot of stuff—quick to compartmentalize and accept things as they were. But unlike me, she never tripped over her own tongue.

That morning, first period was gym class. Back when I was a first-year, I could never be bothered to change into my gym clothes, so I'd just skip class altogether. These days, however, I didn't want to let Shimamura out of my sight, so from now on, I pledged to attend every single class.

Today, all the second-years were gathered outside for a physical fitness test. They divided us into groups and made us run laps on the track, one group at a time, while everyone else sat and waited for their turn.

Shimamura was busy watching the other students run in circles, but *I* was busy watching *her*. This was my first time seeing her in a tracksuit, but somehow it didn't change her aesthetic at all. In fact, I was starting to think she could wear just about anything and it wouldn't matter. Right as I was searching for the words to *describe* said aesthetic, however, a shadow fell over us.

"Ooh, I found Ada-cheechee!"

"Cheechee!"

Hino and Nagafuji ran up to us, Hino pushing Nagafuji along like they were pretending to be a train.

"I see you switched it up this time," Shimamura commented quietly, but I had no idea what she was referring to. "You're looking a little damp there, Nagafuji."

Upon further inspection, sure enough, Nagafuji's hair was wet. She smirked and flipped her hair (although it was too short to really go anywhere). "Yeah, I'm fresh out of the tub."

"You nearly made us late for school. I couldn't even dry my hair all the way, thanks to you," Hino grumbled, scowling. I could see water dripping from Nagafuji's hair onto Hino's scalp.

"You should see Hino's bathtub. It's *huge*!" Nagafuji boasted.

Wait...Hino's bathtub?

Then, as if she'd read my mind, Shimamura asked, "Why would you take a bath at Hino's house?"

"Oh, we had a sleepover last night," Nagafuji replied offhandedly.

What?

To me, this came as something of a shock. She spent the night at Hino's house, then went directly to school the next day? Not only that, but Hino made it sound like they took a bath *together*...

What?!

"Huh," Shimamura replied, mildly disinterested. But Hino looked flustered. She hastily started steering Nagafuji away.

"We can talk about it another time. We gotta go!"

And off they went to rejoin the rest of their group.

"Never a dull moment with those two," Shimamura commented as she watched them go. Then she turned back and gazed out at the athletic field. But I had to put all that stuff on pause for a minute to think. My brain was still processing Nagafuji and Hino's shocking revelation.

A sleepover! Part of me was scandalized, but another part of me was *inspired*. I looked at Shimamura as she stared out at the track. She glanced over.

"Can...can we have one, too?" I asked.

"What?" Her eyes widened, but I kept going.

"A sleepover, I mean?"

"...Huh? At Hino's house?"

"No, no, no!" I shook my head a dozen times. "At...at *your* house!"

Her face froze. Was it really such an absurd request? I could feel myself getting dizzy as I waited for her response. Then she tilted her head. "What for?"

What do you mean, what for???

"Our bathtub's not that big."

"That's not..."

Not important? Really? Okay, on second thought, maybe I *did* care a little. But this was no time to get hung up on small details. It was *way* too early for that.

"...I don't care about the size of your bathtub. I just want to sleep over."

"Hmmmm..." Shimamura closed her eyes and pressed a finger to her forehead. "How come?"

Her question had remained functionally the same, just phrased more gently this time. Granted, I could see how it might be alarming for your friend to spontaneously suggest a sleepover, so I understood why she wasn't very enthusiastic about it...but now that I'd put the idea out there, I couldn't afford to walk it back. There was just no telling when the next opportunity would roll around, and the wait would be agony.

Opportunities are like ice cubes floating in the soda of life. You may think you want a lot of them, but the more you try to add in, the more watered down everything else gets.

"Because...I want to...be friends with you," I admitted. It was a spur-of-the-moment idea, so I sincerely had no other underlying motivations. And now that I had choked out all my Shimamura-related hopes and dreams, sure enough, I was well and truly empty inside.

"Aren't we already friends?" She looked at me wide-eyed, as if to say *this is news to me, pal*.

"Uhh...n-no, yeah, totally! I just...want to be *better* friends," I stammered, averting my eyes. My field of vision narrowed like I was wearing a veil.

For some reason, I just couldn't seem to keep my composure around her...and lately it was getting worse and worse. *I want to be friends with you*—what did that even *mean*? I had no idea, and I was the one who said it!

"So we'll be 'better friends' if you sleep at my house? Is that...how that works?"

Shimamura tilted her head skeptically. But the words were too heavy to take back on a whim. After all, she had a point; even *I* didn't think there was any single prescribed method to deepen a friendship.

"Hmmmm..." She stared out at the athletic field, lost in thought.

Was it simply too soon for us to progress to the Hino-and-Nagafuji stage? One could argue that we needed to work on our friendship a little more first, but at the same time, I didn't think friendship was something you were supposed to "grind," like experience points in an RPG. If there was a checklist of quests to complete to unlock each level, then no one would ever have any problems making friends. But on the other hand, I had to admit, it *did* seem a little absurd to call myself her "best friend" without putting in the time. So what was I supposed to do?

If only we lived in a world where a single hug was all it took to make someone love you.

"Those two are really rubbing off on you, aren't they?" Shimamura said suddenly, turning back to face me. And embarrassingly enough, she was completely right. I buried my chin between my knees and looked up at her.

"Is that a bad thing?"

"It's just super obvious."

That didn't answer my question. Ashamed and anxious, I waited with bated breath for her to make her decision. I sat there, restless, counting the seconds. And then, finally...

"Eh, sure, why not."

Voilà. Just like that, the magic words made all my worries disappear. I was so relieved to hear it, I collapsed forward, slamming my forehead against my kneecaps.

Later that day, after school...

"So, wanna come over at some point this weekend, or...?" Shimamura asked tentatively, checking the calendar app on her phone. I nodded instantly.

We were at the donut shop at the mall, sitting at a table by the window. As it turned out, a fun side perk of sleepover planning was that I got to use it as an excuse to hang out with her after school, too. This was already proving to be *such* a good idea.

"I wanna stay both nights, so...I guess the whole weekend...?"

"*Two nights*? My house isn't a ryokan, you know," Shimamura laughed. "Unlike, say, Hino's place."

"Is Hino's house really that big?"

She hasn't spent the night there before, has she?

"According to Nagafuji, it's a freaking *mansion*. I haven't seen it for myself, though."

Apparently not. Whew. What a relief.

Frankly, I had no interest in Hino's mansion whatsoever. I didn't care how big anyone's house was; I only cared about whether Shimamura was in it.

"I'd just be sitting around at home either way, so...I figured I may as well spend the weekend with you instead," I explained.

"What about your job?"

"I'll still go to work, uh...from your house, I guess."

For some reason, this made Shimamura laugh. *What? What's so funny?* Other people's laughter made me anxious, especially if I didn't know the reason behind it.

"Let's see here..."

She set her phone down and took a bite of her donut;

likewise, I took a bite of mine. She had bought three in total—one for herself and the rest for her sister, or so I had assumed, but...wasn't that kind of a lot for one little girl?

Then she noticed me frowning at her donuts. "I figure there'll be a second one pestering me when I get home," she explained with a self-deprecating laugh. "What is it with me and little sisters? I'm practically starting a collection."

She gazed into the distance, absently wiping off her sugary fingers with a napkin. Then I realized her eyes were fixed on me. Blinking dubiously, I pointed at myself. "Am I one of them?"

"Ha ha ha!"

She laughed at me!

Her playful grin seemed to say *well-spotted, genius*. Normally her smile was only warm enough to get her through the social interaction, but this time I could see it in her eyes, too. It was a heartwarming sight, except...you know...she was still making fun of me.

Glaring down at the table, I ruminated on this.

Shimamura's little sister... Shimamura Sakura... Nice alliteration, I guess.

In a way, it felt like a promotion from ordinary friendship, which was great...but at the same time, if I got *too* close, I had a feeling she'd start to look past me.

I sat cross-legged in the center of my room, gazing around and wondering what to pack first. After all, it couldn't hurt to prepare in advance, right? And besides, I wanted to make sure I had everything I could possibly need so I could avoid any last-minute panicking. Nothing weird about that. Yep, pretty normal.

Honestly, I was just trying to distract myself from my restlessness.

Clean clothes were a must. I counted the number of times I expected to change clothes, then looked down at my splayed fingers and grimaced.

I only had two or three different "lounging at home" shirts, and worse, they were all just color variations of the same shirt. Technically I *did* have some other clothes—the stuff I bought in anticipation of my Christmas date with Shimamura, none of which I ended up wearing, currently gathering dust in the back of my closet. But those were *winter* clothes, so I couldn't really get away with wearing them in the springtime.

I'm gonna have to go shopping again. On my memo pad, I wrote down: *buy new clothes.* Next, I wrote down *toiletries, underwear, socks, wallet,* and *phone, just in case.* Should I bring a blanket? I didn't know if her house had extra sleeping supplies, but in the worst-case scenario, it was warm enough that I could probably sleep without one. Plus, it would take up too much room in my bag. I crossed it off the list.

I stared down at my memo pad. Did I forget anything? The more I wrote, the more it started to look like a vacation checklist. Was this too much? My bag was so full, you'd think I was planning to move in. I folded my arms in contemplation.

There was no point in going to Shimamura's house *just* to sleep. I mean, sure, I would obviously enjoy getting to spend time with her in her natural environment, but I wouldn't want her to get bored. I needed to plan some kind of activity for us, lest we end up sitting there in silence, like that last phone call we had.

What if I packed a game or something? Or a deck of cards? Now it was *really* starting to feel like a vacation. That said, I couldn't think of any two-player card games. What about some other kind of two-player game? Shogi? Othello? I didn't know how to play shogi, but Othello could work. In the corner of the page, I wrote *Othello*.

Then I looked up, and my gaze drifted to the boomerang on display on my shelf. Not that I had any plans of bringing it, but then I thought about ping-pong, and it occurred to me that maybe Shimamura preferred her activities on the physical side. Come to think of it, we went bowling at one point, too. Honestly, I wouldn't mind going again—*without* the little weirdo this time. But if the whole day was spent hanging out downtown, then was there really any point in me sleeping over?

"...Of course there is."

Wouldn't it be fun to leave the house together? To come home together? It sounded so magical. I added *bowling* to my memo.

Okay, what next?

Unfortunately, that was where my momentum came to a halt. What did normal people do with their friends for fun? For a moment, I considered asking Hino or Nagafuji, but something told me they wouldn't be of much help. After all, neither of them could really be described as "normal." Especially Nagafuji. Whatever answer she gave, it probably wouldn't make a lick of sense.

Man, this is complicated. I set my pen down and folded my arms again. It felt like I was trying to solve a paradox.

Knowing Shimamura, she probably wasn't worried about it at all. Sometimes she could be so cold, it made me shiver.

Shimamura... Shimamura's house... Just me and Shimamura...

If we really had no better options, we could always watch TV together. I could sit between her legs, like last time...and then I'd look over my shoulder, and...

I pressed both hands to the floor, hung my head, and waited for the fever to subside. Then, once I regained my composure, I folded my arms again, closed my eyes, and asked myself: would I really be able to stand my ground this time? Could I meet her gaze?

Yeah, I can do it. I won't back down, said a voice in my head. But I knew this was easier said than done. After all, if I paused to imagine what "not backing down" would entail...

All the blood rushed to my head as something inside me came to life.

"I won't back down!"

It was surprisingly easy to shout inside my own house when my parents weren't home. Maybe shouting it had unlocked something in my brain. The words practically rolled off my tongue.

I couldn't stay a coward forever. Going forward, my intention was to be more direct with Shimamura.

Once I decided I was done packing, I looked up at the clock. Now what? The day was still far from over; in fact, time seemed to pass even more slowly than it had back when I was a loner. But on the upside, I was actually looking forward to the future for a change.

My right leg jiggled impatiently as I implored the clock: *Please hurry!*

Then, after a beat, I remembered I needed to go clothes shopping.

"Jeez, how much stuff did you bring?"

This was the first thing Shimamura said to me when she answered the door. I had one bag slung over my left shoulder, one on my right shoulder, and a backpack on my back. Surely three wasn't *that* many...right?

"Are you sure you're not planning to move in?" she laughed, and I got the sense she was wondering what exactly I had brought.

After giving it a lot of thought, I decided it would be rude to rely on her family too much, so I brought my own shampoo and conditioner, plus enough food for four days so her parents wouldn't have to cook for me, as well as a blanket. My anxiety refused to be quelled until I accounted for every little possibility, which is how I ended up with bag #2. Then, since I was planning to sleep over Sunday night and walk to school with Shimamura on Monday morning, I realized I needed to pack my textbooks and uniform, hence bag #3.

"Also, aren't you kind of early?"

Rubbing her eyes, she squinted against the morning sun, which illuminated the post-yawn tear tracks on her cheeks. Current time: 8:00 AM.

"Oh, sorry. Were you still asleep?"

Personally, I hadn't been able to get a wink of sleep last night. I laid there for hours. And then the next thing I knew, I was here.

"Mm-hmm. You woke me up. Oh, but I'm not mad or anything. I know you're the super-punctual type! I'm proud of you."

"Uhh...yeah..."

Truth be told, I actually got here at about 7:00, but I figured that was way too early, so instead I rode my bike around the neighborhood for an hour. Fortunately, since it was springtime, I could safely kill time outside without freezing to death. And since it was the weekend, there were no grade-schoolers around to give me funny looks, thank god.

Shimamura ran a hand through her disheveled bangs. "Okay, I think that's all the questions I had," she shrugged, now sounding fully awake. Then she smiled. "Well, come on in!"

And so, like a dog on command, I entered my owner's house. As I took off my shoes, I glanced up—and made eye contact with Shimamura's little sister, standing at the opposite end of the hall. She flinched. I flinched, too.

"This is my friend. Do you remember her?" Shimamura called, introducing me.

I bowed my head. "Th-thanks for having me over."

"Hi," said a tiny voice in reply.

I seemed to remember Shimamura telling me her sister was shy around strangers—same as me. I felt a slight kinship with her.

Then it hit me: was *that* why Shimamura saw me as a little sister?

Meanwhile, Little Shimamura ran off into another room—probably the kitchen.

"As usual, she's pretending to behave herself," Shimamura laughed as she watched her sibling disappear. Then she looked back at me. "Wanna put your stuff upstairs? It's basically the only room that's free."

She pointed at the stairs, and I nearly nodded...but then I remembered: Shimamura's room was on the first floor.

This discontentment must have shown on my face, because she tilted her head and asked, "Do you not like that room?"

"Oh, no, I'm fine with it..." My eyes (and heart) went back and forth as I debated whether to be honest with her. In the end, the words came out anyway: "I just... thought I'd be sleeping in your room."

I'm scared of being alone at night, my brain suggested as an excuse. But if she stopped to consider my family situation, the lie would become all too obvious. She would see right through it.

"So you want to sleep in our room with us?" she asked, without being coy or beating around the bush.

If I was being honest, the answer was *yes, please.* I shot her a hopeful look. But Shimamura smiled sadly, like she was conflicted.

"As much as I'd love that, I don't think my sister would be cool with it. Sorry."

"Oh, no worries. It's cool," I blurted out reflexively, forcing a laugh in the hopes that it would keep the massive devastation from showing on my face. No matter how many times life showed me that I couldn't expect to get every single thing I wanted, somehow my heart never got the memo.

First things first, Shimamura sent me upstairs to drop my stuff off...in the same room where we had previously studied together. Now that winter was over, the kotatsu table had been packed away, and in its place was a single futon, all laid out for me. I set my bags down, then plopped down cross-legged in the middle of the room and reflected on the conversation we just had.

I'd love that, she said.

"She'd love that...?"

Suddenly, the whole world felt a tiny bit brighter. Maybe I was more of a natural optimist than I realized. I took a big, cheerful lungful of air—and it was so dusty, it dried out my sinuses instantly, just like last time. *Maybe I should open the curtains.* I started to get up, then changed my mind and stopped halfway.

Just then, the door opened slightly, and Shimamura peeked in through the gap.

"Do you want breakfast, or did you already eat?"

"Oh, don't worry about me. I packed my own food." I dug through my blue bag and pulled out a package of breadsticks. I'd packed them near the top, so they were only slightly crushed. *Perfect.* "See?"

This way, my presence wouldn't be too much of a burden on her family.

"Oh, really..."

"Yeah."

I blinked, confused, at the awkward pause this seemed to create. Then, right as I went to open the package, Shimamura's eyes widened. "Wait...you're going to eat them up here?"

"Huh?"

"I was thinking maybe you'd come eat with me, like,

in the kitchen? Because I'm about to have breakfast right now."

Ohhhh. It all clicked. *Yeah, that's a much better idea.*

"Oh, no, yeah, totally."

Breadsticks in hand, I hastily got to my feet, and Shimamura laughed at me for being clueless. Story of my life.

She led me back downstairs to the kitchen, where both her sister *and* her mother were seated at the table.

"Come on in," Mrs. Shimamura greeted me, using the exact same words as her daughter and nearly the exact same voice, too. "You can sit right there."

I did as requested, while Shimamura took a seat next to her sister on a different side of the table. In a way, it felt like I was filling in for Shimamura's dad.

"You know, this is the first time we've ever had a sleepover at the house!" Mrs. Shimamura remarked.

Her gaze made me shrink back, but on the inside, I was excited to be the first. Joy welled up inside me. *The first!*

"Too bad it's not a study party, though. Oh, if only," she sighed dramatically, though the grin on her face told me she wasn't actually disappointed.

Granted, a study party would probably make more sense for students our age, since we were generally more focused on school. For a minute I was scared she was going to ask me what our plans were, since I had no idea how to answer that, but luckily she didn't.

I glanced over to find Little Shimamura poking at her omelet and looking vaguely uncomfortable, with her shoulders hunched around her ears. The culprit? My presence. I stared down at the table and opened my package of breadsticks.

"Now, now, Adachi-chan, I made enough for you, too, you know!" Mrs. Shimamura told me as she cheerfully scooted a plate in my direction. Scrambled eggs with toast. "Or is my cooking beneath you, princess?"

"Oh, no, not at all! Thank you very much!"

I quickly set aside my breadsticks and accepted the plate. It was the first time someone had ever playfully pressured me into eating their food.

I took a tiny nibble of toast and glanced back at Little Shimamura. She, too, was nibbling. Then our eyes met, and I hastily stared down at the table. Unlike her mother, Little Shimamura didn't seem too keen on welcoming me into the house. Honestly, the feeling was relatable. She and I were clearly cut from the same cloth.

After all, we both wanted her big sister all to ourselves.

"So tell me, Adachi-chan. I'm guessing you're a more competent student than my daughter, is that right?" Mrs. Shimamura asked me.

I glanced at Shimamura and hesitated. "No, I, uh..."

"She's like me, Mom," Shimamura answered in my place.

Yeah, I'm like her. Actually, if anything, I'm probably worse.

"Really? But you seem like such a good girl! More so than this *delinquent*, anyway."

"Will you shut up?" Shimamura snapped, looking uncomfortable. Then she started wolfing down her food, as if to suggest that she didn't want to be in the room for a single moment longer than necessary. Her mother noticed this but didn't seem to care...so I decided to vouch for her.

"If anyone's a good girl, it's Shimamura. She's way, *way* better than me."

It felt a little patronizing to call her a *good girl*, but I couldn't think of any other way to put it. Good *student*? Good *person*? Nothing sounded right in my head.

"Ha ha ha! Oh, I get it! You see her as your little sister, is that it?" Mrs. Shimamura clapped her hands together in complete misunderstanding.

"No, she does *not*," Shimamura hissed, but her mother was laughing too hard to hear her. Apparently my attempt to correct the record had completely backfired.

She stuffed her toast into her mouth, let out a muffled "thanksh for breakfasht" with her cheeks puffed out, and stormed out of the kitchen. Was she mad at me? Feeling guilty, I raced through the rest of my food, chewing at lightning speed and swallowing faster than I probably should have.

"Thank you for the food, ma'am." When was the last time I actually thanked the person who cooked for me?

At this, Mrs. Shimamura started laughing again. "You're like two peas in a pod!"

Next, I carried my dirty plate to the sink to wash it, but she hurried after me.

"Don't worry about it," she told me. "Though I wish that lazy daughter of mine would take a leaf out of your book," she added with a sigh. I didn't know how to respond to that, so I nodded vaguely. Then I waved goodbye, left the kitchen, and chased after Shimamura.

"Are you mad?" I asked.

"Huh? About what?" She turned back to face me. Her expression was no longer sulky, and her voice was back to normal. "Oh, you mean just now? My mom's *always* like that. Getting mad at her is just a waste of time."

She laughed and waved a hand dismissively, not a trace of resentment to be seen.

To me, their mother-daughter relationship was a complicated one, and I couldn't relate whatsoever. But part of me found it fascinating, so I did my best to try to understand it.

"Anyway, more importantly..." Shimamura stared directly into my eyes, cradling her arm and smiling faintly. "What's on the agenda for today?"

Her voice tickled my ears as the curtain officially rose on our weekend plans. A muddled mixture of hope and panic spurred me onward.

How long had it been since I last looked forward to the weekend?

Wait, what the?

It was bedtime, and as I stared up at the ceiling, a question suddenly came to me:

What on earth did we do all day long?

There really wasn't much worth mentioning. I spent the day hovering over Shimamura, just like always, except this time I got to do it for a lot longer than usual. We played Othello...then we watched TV (sitting side by side on our knees for some reason)...then I showed Shimamura everything I'd brought with me, and she laughed and shook her head at me. I was overly enthusiastic, but she was not; she simply let things happen, same as any other day.

Every now and then I'd catch her staring into space, her eyes drooping lethargically. Then she'd notice me looking at her, and a smile would slowly creep up onto her face. Her delayed reactions made some part of me seize up internally, and until I figured out what part it was, I got the feeling it would haunt me.

Long story short, it was just an ordinary day like any other.

In a sense, "just being together for no reason" was what I wanted more than anything, but another part of me had hoped that something dramatic would happen, and I still needed some time before I could bridge the gap between the two.

Had I really wasted the entire day doing nothing?

Well...if I had to say...there *was* this one thing that happened...

"Once you finish eating, get your butt in the tub. You always fall into a food coma right after dinner," Mrs. Shimamura told her daughter at the dinner table.

"Yes, Moooom," Shimamura replied offhandedly. Then she shot me a quick glance, like she was embarrassed that I had to witness the exchange. Normally *I* was the one who was constantly embarrassed, so for me, this was a fun change of pace.

After that, I was surprised to learn that Mrs. Shimamura had made enough food for me, too, without me even having to ask.

This was also the point at which I encountered Shimamura's dad for the first time since I got there. He fixed me with a winning smile and said, "A charming young lady like you would brighten up any dinner table." At this, Shimamura cringed, but I figured it was some kind of dad joke. Either that, or I had just discovered where his daughter got her natural charm.

After dinner, instead of retreating to her own room, Shimamura automatically followed me upstairs. The gesture warmed my heart and filled me with a strange sense of superiority—over whom, I couldn't say, but I felt like a god.

Newly emboldened, I asked her: "Can I, um, sit between your legs?"

How had I asked this question last time around? Had I gotten a little more confident since then? Granted, I had no memory of what happened last time, so I couldn't say for sure, but I somehow doubted I'd made any progress.

Meanwhile, Shimamura's lips curled in a devilish smirk. "Only if you promise not to run away this time."

Oof.

She spread her legs for me in a V-shape. Timidly, I sat down cross-legged between them, gazing at them all the while. Her legs were really beautiful; honestly, she'd probably look better in my *cheongsam* than I did. *Now there's something I'd like to see.*

"Aren't you going to lean up against me?" Shimamura asked, patting her chest invitingly, just like last time.

"Okay then, if you don't mind..."

Hesitantly, I leaned back against her. My eyes flew open.

Aaaa...whaaa...eeee...!

...Times like these, I was honestly such a creep. Or maybe I was just plain stupid. My face flushed beet red as I felt...you know, her boobs...press up against my back. Now that we were in T-shirts instead of our stiff, starchy uniforms, I could feel them a lot more clearly...especially when she leaned forward to match my posture... My pulse raced and my eyes darted in all directions as I tried desperately to keep myself from babbling.

Why? Why do I always end up like this? I just couldn't understand it. Shimamura and I were both girls. Why would I care if her boobs were pressed up against me? My hands fidgeted restlessly atop my thighs.

As I sat there and screamed internally, it wasn't long before I heard what sounded like faint, rhythmic snoring.

Was she asleep? I wanted to glance over my shoulder and check, but what if I woke her up? I froze more stiffly than ever before as I held my breath. Apparently Shimamura wasn't kidding when she said she spent her weekends sleeping.

Then I felt her lie down onto her back on the floor, and as her warmth was replaced with cold, empty air, I felt my spirits deflate somewhat. That said, I was acting like a total freak. *It's probably for the best,* I told myself, forcing myself to accept it.

So there we were, Shimamura sprawled out on the floor with her legs splayed, and me sitting criss-cross applesauce in between them. Kind of surreal. As I gazed down at her, I remembered Mrs. Shimamura's comment from earlier and chuckled to myself. She knew her daughter all too well... Classic mom stuff.

Thinking about it, my mom was no exception, either. She at least knew me well enough to know that I was indecipherable.

Just then, the door opened, and a little head peeked in. This seemed to wake Shimamura, because I felt her legs twitch.

It was her sister, of course. She looked at us and narrowed her eyes. In her little hands was a change of clothes—pajamas, if I had to guess. Shimamura took one look at her and somehow intuited that she was going to take a shower.

"You don't normally take your bath so early," she commented to her younger sibling, who ignored her and walked into the room.

Then she turned her little face away and announced, "I want you to come with me, Nee-chan."

"I beg your pardon?"

At this, Shimamura sat upright. Likewise, I wasn't expecting this, either.

"Where did that come from? I thought you said you were too old to take a bath with me anymore."

"We can still do it *sometimes*. Now come on!"

Little Shimamura took her nee-chan by the hand. Reluctantly, Shimamura pushed herself onto her feet, stooped over slightly, as Little Shimamura dragged her away. She glanced back at me. "I...uh...I'll be back in a bit, apparently!"

And with that, she left the room. With my back support now gone, I wrapped my arms around my bent knees and rolled over onto my side like a Daruma doll.

Right before they left the room, Little Shimamura had shot me a look over her shoulder. A very pronounced scowl, to be specific. And I knew *exactly* what had caused that scowl and why. Thus, I couldn't bring myself to stop them, nor could I join them. It was like she had held up a mirror, and I'd lost myself in its reflection.

So yeah, that happened.

The two of us were similar, right down to our faults, so it was only natural that we wouldn't get along without some fine-tuning. And for the record, I *did* want to get along with her, if possible. But if that meant I had to sacrifice certain things regarding her big sister, then it wasn't the right move, and I was only interested in making the right moves. *I already screw up enough as it is, thanks.*

"First she gets to take a bath with her, and then they get to sleep in the same bed... Okay, maybe not the same bed, but definitely the same room..."

I couldn't help but feel somewhat jealous of her. After all, her status as "blood-related little sister" meant she was fully allowed to be needy and demanding, no questions asked. She was practically invincible.

I stared up into the darkness, wide awake. Tonight, the usual veil of drowsiness was nowhere to be found.

Yeah, this is gonna be a long night.

Then, as I was lying there, it belatedly occurred to me: nighttime took up more than 50 percent of each day.

What was the point in me spending more than half the weekend all alone? Shimamura-wise, it just didn't make sense. (Not that "Shimamura-wise" makes a lot of sense either, but let's not worry about that.)

The bottom line was this: I had come here to spend time with Shimamura, and yet here I was, wasting the majority of said time being apart from her. It was defeating half the purpose. And only now, at the end of the day, had I finally put two and two together. The phrase "hindsight is 20/20" came to mind.

This was why I decided to take action while there was still time. Tomorrow was another day, after all. But this was the part I needed to change about myself. This was the part I needed to work on. And with conviction thus renewed in my heart—

"...Nnngh..."

—there was no way I was falling asleep anytime soon.

Regret set in.

I really should've saved this revelation for the morning instead.

As anyone who's ever had a job could tell you, you don't exactly get to pick your days off...and the next day,

I was scheduled to work the lunch shift. Yes, it would eat into my time with Shimamura, but it wasn't all bad.

"Have fun at work," a very bed-headed Shimamura mumbled sleepily as she saw me off. Instantly, what was once an ordinary front door was now a powerful portal. Somehow it filled me with both courage and reluctance simultaneously. A slight warmth descended into my stomach.

"Um...I'll be back soon."

The warmth rained down on me from behind, soaking me gently.

"I...I got this!"

I raised both fists in the air. At first Shimamura's eyes widened, but then she covered her mouth and giggled. It was rare for my jokes to actually land, so perhaps this was a sign that today was going to be a good day.

With a spring in my step, I strolled down the street. A cloudless blue sky hung above me. *Yep, today's a good day.* Meanwhile, I thought about what had put that spring in my step to begin with.

Why had that little exchange felt so thrilling? Well, probably because I didn't have the best relationship with my family. But if I put in the effort, could things be different? Part of me figured it was probably too late, but another part of me had watched the Shimamura family and come away inspired to try.

And so I arrived at work, where absolutely nothing had changed with the passing of the seasons. Same coworkers, same stupid *cheongsam*. But ever since Shimamura told me I looked good in it, I found I didn't really mind wearing it anymore.

As I waited for customers to arrive, I tugged the hem down. Sure, I didn't *mind* wearing the dress, but I wasn't *comfortable* in it. It was hard to explain, but...even though my school uniform revealed a lot more leg, comparatively speaking, somehow it was still preferable to this *cheongsam*. Not sure why.

Fifteen minutes after we opened for the lunch rush, the first group of customers arrived, followed by another customer on her own. My body moved on autopilot. Preparing the oshibori towels, filling the water cups—it was all mindless busywork to me. I had no motive to keep going, but no reason to stop, either. And so it continued ad nauseum.

I set a glass of water down on the solo customer's table. I recited my stock line: "Let me know when you're ready to order."

But right as I turned to leave...

"Huh?"

The girl looked up from her menu and stared at me, but not in a "ready to order" sort of way. I froze, unsure what to do. Then she smiled.

"I knew it! It *is* you! You're the girl who found my strap for me!"

She hoisted her bookbag up and flipped it over to show me the little cartoon bear hanging from it. Sure enough, I recognized it as the same strap I rescued at the mall that one day...and incidentally, it was the very same strap Shimamura had as well.

Then I realized: it was the girl from the pet shop.

"That was really cool of you, by the way. Thanks again."

"Oh, uh, no problem."

Just then, I remembered I'd been wanting to get a matching set of...something...for me and Shimamura. Maybe we could go shopping together after I got back... Somehow it felt like I was full of good ideas today. Perhaps it was a side benefit of sleeping over at the Shimamura house. *Yeah, that's gotta be it,* my brain decided optimistically.

"Oh my *god*, your face!"

"Huh?"

I snapped back to my senses to find the girl staring at me slack-jawed. Hastily, I pressed my face back into position with my hands. *What? What's wrong with it?* Terrified, my gaze darted in all directions.

"I thought maybe you had resting bitch face, but clearly I was wrong!" she laughed, rubbing it in further.

Part of me was scared to ask, but at the same time, not knowing was far scarier. "Wh-what was wrong with it?"

"Umm...it looked kinda...melty?"

"What?"

"Like it was falling apart, like..." She tugged the bottom half of her face downwards until her mouth looked...well...melty.

"...Really?"

"Yeah."

"...Let me know when you're ready to order," I choked, clinging to the last scraps of my professionalism. Then I hurried away as fast as my legs could carry me.

My ears were ringing as I grabbed a plate and started polishing. Like a mirror, it reflected my shame right back at me.

After work, I stood at the door to Shimamura's house and contemplated what to say as I walked inside. I didn't live here, so it would be weird to say "I'm home." Granted, whenever I returned to my actual house, I never said anything at all, since no one was ever home around that timeframe. Ultimately, I decided to go with the same thing I'd said last time I entered, even if it was kind of odd to repeat.

"Thanks for having me..."

"Oh, welcome home."

As it happened, Mrs. Shimamura was kneeling right there in the entryway, cleaning the floor. The instantaneous reply shocked me. *Welcome home,* she said. My throat tightened. Then she gave me a funny look, and I knew I needed to say something.

"Th-thank you very much."

Like an idiot, I thanked her *again.* But she didn't really seem to notice.

"Hougetsu's not home at the moment. I think she said she was going shopping."

"Oh, I see..."

For a moment, I wasn't sure who she was talking about, but then I remembered. That was Shimamura's first name—and what a name it was, too. It was so dignified, it was almost impossible to make it sound cute. Hougetsu-chan? Hou-chan?

"She'll be home soon. She's lazy, so she'll want to get it over with as fast as possible."

"Right..."

"She's always been an oversleeper, right from birth. I swear, she sleeps like a koala," Mrs. Shimamura sighed wistfully. Meanwhile, I nodded along awkwardly. Without Shimamura here, I felt extremely out of place.

Please come home now. Please, please, please.

"What's she like at school?" Mrs. Shimamura continued.

"What do you mean?"

She looked up from scrubbing the floor. "Does she go to class?"

"Yes, ma'am."

"Well, alright then." She was so quick to shrug off the conversation—just like her daughter. "It must be a struggle, trying to get that lazybones to keep up with you."

What?

"No, no, not at all. If anything, um, it's the other way around."

"Oh?"

"Shimamura's always guiding me along, you know, like a...like a leash." That was probably a weird metaphor, but I couldn't think of anything better.

Mrs. Shimamura laughed like I was joking. "Now *there's* a surprise!" Her smile was nearly identical to her daughter's.

Just then, as if on cue, the door opened. *Speak of the devil and she doth appear.*

"I'm hoooome!" Shimamura called. Then she spotted me and immediately changed tack. "Oh, hey, Adachi. Welcome back." A small paper shopping bag hung from her hand.

"Thanks."

"You're welcome." Then she spotted her mother in the entryway. She looked back at me. "You guys weren't talking about me, were you?"

"Keh heh heh!" Mrs. Shimamura cackled.

Shimamura narrowed her eyes but didn't press further. Instead, she took her shoes off.

"Hmm..." She looked down the hallway, then at the staircase. "Eh, upstairs it is." And so she headed up the stairs.

Naturally, I followed after her. Maybe my leash metaphor was more accurate than I realized, because I felt like a puppy chasing after my owner.

Once we stepped into the study room, Shimamura let out a sigh. "Ugh. God." Right as she started to play with her hair, however, she seemed to remember something. "Oh, that's right!" She turned to me and smiled brightly. "Adachi, bend down for a sec!"

"Huh...? Okay..."

I crouched down as requested, and a shadow fell over my eyes as Shimamura reached out and touched my hair. *What the?*

"There we go."

She had taken something out of her shopping bag and now she was affixing it to my head. Once she was all done, she took a step back to admire her handiwork.

"There! Now we have the same hairstyle."

"Huh?"

Shimamura grabbed a hand mirror and held it up so I could see. Reflected back at me was a girl with pink cheeks—that part was nothing new—and a flower hairpin on the right side of my bangs. Sure enough, our hairstyles now matched. Was this what she went out to buy?

"Now that my hair's almost as dark as yours, I've been wanting to try matching hairstyles with you, but... Hmm. I guess it's not quite the same."

She peered at my face so intently, I couldn't help but stare at the floor in embarrassment. Where did this come from? Times like these, she really reminded me of her dad.

Regardless of her motive, however, I was touched that she would go out of her way to buy me a gift. It was a gesture that took effort—effort that Shimamura didn't always want to put in—and that was why it meant so much.

As I ran a finger over this new symbol of our friendship, Shimamura looked up suddenly. "Oh, right. So, I actually bought two of those. One for you, and one for me."

"...Huh?"

Shimamura had bought herself the same hairpin? So... we could match? Was it because I'd asked about it? She sounded pretty casual about it, so maybe she wasn't all that invested. Or maybe she didn't even remember me saying I wanted to match with her at all. Still...that was all it took to set off fireworks inside my brain. Glittering sparks flew in every direction, making me lightheaded. And yet at the same time, I was filled with an indescribable sense of euphoria. I trembled internally.

"Sh-Shimamura...!"

"Grrk!"

I threw myself onto her so fast, I nearly knocked her head clean off her shoulders. But I couldn't stop myself.

"You're just so...!"

"Hmm, this feels familiar."

"So *grape*!"

Right as I attempted to profess my feelings, however, I accidentally bit my tongue.

"I'm so...grape? Yum. Is that your favorite flavor?"

The only "flavor" I could taste right now was my own blood. I composed myself, then tried again.

"You're so *great*."

Somehow my tongue was never there for me when I needed it most.

"We already did this little joke before, remember?"

"Yeah..."

I gave her one final squeeze, then let go. Shimamura was smiling, but it wasn't a warm or gentle smile—more like she was trying desperately not to laugh. Then she put her hand to her chin and scrutinized me.

"Hmmm. Nice."

What?

"I like that look on your face." She was now the second person to comment on my face today. My confusion must've been obvious, because she continued, "It's kinda stretched out, you know?"

No, I don't know, actually. I couldn't picture this at all. Stretched in what direction? And for that matter, why did everyone keep critiquing(?) my face lately? Was it really that weird-looking at all hours of the day? If so, this was news to me. Unfortunately, I had no way of checking for myself... Then again, maybe I didn't need to. After all, Shimamura probably wouldn't comment on it if it wasn't true.

"...Well, whatever. Don't worry about it."

"You sure?"

Shimamura tilted her head curiously as I grabbed her by the shoulders and sat her down with me. Thinking about the flower in my hair warmed my heart, but at the same time I was scared my face would melt again, and I needed my expression to be serious for the request I was about to make of her.

"...What's up, Adachi?"

Today, I had vowed to spend more of the day with Shimamura—but it was already nighttime. The sun had started to set, and naturally, it would be a long time before it rose again. And last night, I had discovered that the most important part of spending the night together... was *spending the night together*.

"Shimamura?"

"Yeah?"

"Would you wanna sleep together this time?" My molars throbbed painfully. My eyes stung, and I realized I was forgetting to blink again. "Just... wondering..."

Then I shrank into my shoulders like a scolded child and timidly awaited her answer.

I was constantly torn between my fear of rejection and my desperate need to get the words out at any cost. And in the tug-of-war between optimism and pessimism, optimism generally prevailed. But by no means did this mean I had defeated my own shortcomings—not by a long shot. The only winner here was Shimamura.

"Sure, I don't mind," she shrugged casually.

For a minute I questioned whether I was dreaming, but the pin swaying with my bangs informed me otherwise. But there was no rush of joy, no feeling of accomplishment. Somehow it didn't even register that she'd said yes.

I mean, if it was *that easy*, then...then...

"I should've..."

"Should've what?"

I should've suggested it last night!

A whirlwind of regret whipped around me. I never imagined she would agree to it so readily... Sometimes she could be bizarrely accepting of the strangest things. Like me sitting between her legs. Was she like this with everyone? She was impossible to read, which was why I screwed up so much.

But sometimes, right when I least expected it, she would be there to catch me when I stumbled. And those moments were pure bliss.

That night, I scrubbed my body so thoroughly, you'd think I was trying to physically erase myself. By the end, my skin was practically raw.

"It feels like I always screw something up..."

As I sat cross-legged on my futon, burning with self-loathing and cursing my idiocy, Shimamura walked in...carrying a second futon.

Wait, what?

"Wait, what?"

Oops. Said it out loud.

"What's up?" Shimamura asked curiously as she laid out her bedding next to mine.

In a way, it added to the "vacation" feel of the sleepover, but, uh...I kinda thought we were going to be sharing the same futon. I couldn't bring myself to say it out loud, however.

I shook my head. "Nothing."

Clearly I was getting too greedy. I tucked my knees up to my shin in shame. Meanwhile, Shimamura flopped down onto her futon with her limbs splayed in every direction. Her skin was faintly flushed, suggesting she was fresh out of the tub herself. Did her little sister join her again? The thought made me feel almost...*defeated*, in a way.

Could Shimamura and I ever get to the point where we could take a bath together? How long would it take for her to feel that comfortable with me? The road ahead felt long and narrow and treacherous.

...To be clear, I didn't want to see her naked or anything like that. Obviously. I wasn't a creep. But my desires were complicated. While my need for physical affection was driven purely by a lack of emotional fulfillment, ultimately it was still physical... *Ugh, what am I even talking about right now?*

I glanced at her out of the corner of my eye. "So, uh, is she okay with it?"

She looked over at me without sitting up. "Is who okay with what?"

"Your sister. Is she cool with you sleeping up here?" Admittedly, I felt a little guilty for essentially stealing Shimamura away.

"*Ohhhh*. Yeah, she's fine," she replied with a knowing smile. "She's got a little sleepover of her own going on down there."

With who? The little blue-haired girl? Supposedly she came over to the Shimamura house all the time these days. Who even *was* she, anyway? No one in the Shimamura family seemed to find her odd, so I shrugged it off, but... how could she possibly have *blue hair*?

Considering Little Shimamura was so buddy-buddy with her, perhaps it was proof that she was just as weird as her nee-chan.

I snuck a furtive glance at Shimamura lying unguarded on her futon. Not that I had any room to talk, but...man, she could be really odd sometimes. Maybe sharing a room with her little sister had trained her in the ways of weirdos... Was *that* why she saw me as a little sister?

If it really, truly made me special to her, then I could accept it. But Shimamura already *had* a little sister, and

I couldn't possibly compete with the real deal. I knew I couldn't stay complacent forever...but tonight, I was going to make the most of it.

"So, uh, Shimamura...w-wanna call it a night?" I suggested, still sitting upright, without even looking at the clock.

"Already?!" Shimamura asked, surprised. "But it's only 8!"

"Huh? Oh...you're right..."

I checked the time, and sure enough, it was 7:50. To me, it felt like it was practically midnight. I was ready to hit the sack.

"Work really wore me out today, and I can't stop yawning, so I guess I just figured I'm probably sleepy, so I thought it was time for bed! Oh, and we have school tomorrow, so we don't want to oversleep!"

As I tried to argue my case, I got a bit worked up. And if I had to guess, this probably backfired on me. She gave me a funny look. "You sound like you're wide awake."

I slumped my shoulders. I couldn't argue with that. And after that panic, I was actually tired now.

"That said, I could probably fall asleep just fine." She squeezed her eyes shut, and her face relaxed.

This was quite possibly my first time bearing witness to Shimamura's favorite hobby: sleeping. On the one hand, I was happy to learn more about her, but on the other hand...how would this information help me?

"Alright, time for bed!" she shrugged. I glanced over to find her halfway to her feet. "Not like there's anything better to do, anyway." With that, she reached up and grabbed the ceiling light cord. "Ready for lights out? Need to use the restroom or anything?"

"Uh...nah, I'm set..."

"Okay then, good night!" The light clicked off, and Shimamura slid under the covers.

"Good night," I mumbled back, but I wasn't sure she heard me.

The conversation ended there, and after a long moment, I found myself wondering: *Wait...are we really going to sleep?* I felt like a disembodied head, keenly conscious of everything from the neck up.

Then I laid myself down...and started rolling.

Could I excuse it away by claiming I rolled around a lot in my sleep? I seriously considered this option, but... the answer was *no, probably not*. I could try it, but I wouldn't get away with it...and for a variety of reasons.

Was this the most I could reasonably expect? Was I meant to be satisfied by merely lying *next* to her? Obviously I couldn't bridge these gaps immediately... The words "let's be realistic" came to mind.

But I shook them away.

There was nothing wrong with taking a realistic approach, per se, but it was silly to throw your dreams away in pursuit of 100 percent realism. What's the point of living, if not for your dreams? That's not living at all—that's just inertia.

I sat up slightly and looked over at Shimamura. She was breathing rhythmically with her eyes closed... Was she asleep already? Stealthily, I slipped out from under my blanket. Then, crawling on all fours, I carefully approached her and peered down at her from up close. Squinting through the darkness, I admired her face—beautiful and still, like a sculpture. My eyes drifted to her lips, and I felt my cheeks burn.

Oh, how dearly I wished she would invite me to cuddle.

For the record, I wasn't planning to do anything *weird*. I was just looking at her. The memory of a distant dream flashed through my mind, and my heart skipped a beat. But again, I wasn't going to do anything risky. Not without any guarantees.

See? Look at that—she opened her eyes.

Wait, what? Oh god, she opened her eyes???

For a moment, we stared at each other in the dark.

"Need something?"

Apparently my mere presence had woken her. Now she was giving me a weird look.

All I have to do is stay calm and explain. I haven't done anything inappropriate, nor was I planning to. I'm perfectly innocent.

"I was just...wondering if you were actually asleep."

"Uh, yeah! I'm in bed, aren't I? Silly." She laughed.

Right, of course. I moved to scoot back...but my hands and knees were glued to the floor.

"...Adachi?"

My body was pitching a fit and refusing to cooperate... possibly because my mind kept lingering on that uncomfortably vivid imagery. For some reason, I just couldn't bring myself to widen the distance between us.

Three, two, one...go!

I willed myself to move. But this willpower didn't spring up voluntarily. I had to give it a motivating kick in the rear. *Useless.*

I craned my neck forward...and plunged myself face-first onto Shimamura's futon. A dull pain rose up from my flattened nose.

"What are you, a mosquito?" I heard her ask somewhere above me. But when I summoned the courage to lift my head, I found her face was a lot closer than I was expecting.

"Can we...c-cuddle?" I stammered bluntly, without beating around the bush. No more waiting around. This time, I was taking my life into my own hands.

Shimamura stared back at me, stone-faced. "Now I get it," she murmured. *What? What did she get?*

But before I could panic, she pulled the blanket back invitingly. I looked at her: *you sure?* She rolled over onto her side, facing me, and beckoned for me to join her.

This was not a dream; the pain in my nose was proof of that. If I had a tail, I would've been wagging it a hundred miles a minute.

I flopped down like a dead fish and clumsily rolled under her blanket. My dry, unmoisturized skin kept catching on the fabric, and the bottom left quadrant of my body had already gone numb. But there we were, inches apart, facing each other. If I wasn't careful, I was in danger of babbling like an idiot.

Then Shimamura smirked, and it was both so sudden and so close in proximity that it affected me even more strongly than usual.

"Wh-what?"

"My little sister did this *exact* same thing last night."

"...Oh..." In the darkness, I burned with shame at the thought that I had inadvertently imitated a grade-schooler.

"And then she asked for *this*, too."

Shimamura reached out and slid her arm under my head. I felt her warmth against my cheek and belatedly realized: she was letting me use her arm as a pillow.

"How's that? Is it comfy, laying on your onee-chan's arm?" she teased.

It was like a dream come true, and I hadn't even had the dream yet. Was this what they called sheer ecstasy? Enraptured, I struggled to find my words.

"I think..."

"You think...?"

"I think I might cry," I admitted weakly.

Shimamura smiled and shook her head at me, as if to say *it's not that deep*. But while I may have seemed over-emotional, it was actually quite the opposite. At last, I was at peace.

"I feel so relaxed. Like all my stiff muscles have finally unclenched." And this, in turn, gave my emotions free rein over me, hence the waterworks.

"Is it really that big of a deal?" she asked. I nodded. But she didn't seem uncomfortable with my tears. She looked at my hair. "Your hair's still damp, you know."

"Uh huh." At the time, I was too panicked to be thorough...but that panic felt distant now.

"There's something special about damp warmth that feels really nice," she mused. As she stroked my hair, the beads of water transferred to her fingers. Little beads of contentment. "Okay, can I have my arm back now?"

"Not yet."

I clung to her pajamas like a spoiled child. She looked down at the desperation in my fingers and let out a sigh. "How much longer do you need?"

"Just until I fall asleep," I replied, wide-eyed.

Honestly, I didn't feel even remotely sleepy. I didn't *need* to sleep—I was already living out my wildest dreams.

"You're *hopeless*, you know that?" Shimamura smirked wryly, her voice gentle and soothing. But she didn't pull her arm away.

There we were, lying side by side, breathing faintly in the dark. Now that my eyes had adjusted, I could see everything that truly mattered to me.

"Oh, that's right. The seating shuffle's tomorrow," Shimamura remarked offhandedly.

To her, this small detail was incidental at most, but to me, it came as a shock. "Wait, what?"

Shimamura looked at me in confusion for a moment, but then it seemed to click. "*Ohhhh*, that's right. You were cutting class the day we found out."

"Oh, okay."

Makes sense... Then my eyes flew open. *A seating shuffle?! Tomorrow?! I won't even have time to pray!*

"Adachi?"

I wanted to be closer to Shimamura, even if only by a single step. Or a single inch. But what if I ended up at the very front and she ended up in the very back?

"Well, uh…hopefully they let us sit this close! Right?"

For some reason, I wanted her to give me…reassurance or validation or something like that. But Shimamura laughed it off.

"I don't know about that. I feel like it would cause a lot of problems." She was always perfectly composed; not once had I ever seen her get flustered. "I mean, to get *this* close, we'd basically have to share a desk, you know?"

This came as a small, but crushing, blow. I just couldn't accept her flippant tone.

But I must've let these feelings show on my face, because she looked at me and continued, "Whatever happens, happens."

This outlook was certainly in line with Shimamura's personality, and there was nothing wrong with it, per se. But if I let life just *happen* to me, I knew I'd end up alone again. So I took a good, hard look at my fears and motivations…and after a little introspection, the answer came to me right away. Regardless of how the seating shuffle turned out—

"Wanna eat lunch together tomorrow?"

—all we had to do was make our own plans. It was so simple, and yet somehow I never realized.

"Yeah, of course."

And so Shimamura readily agreed, putting me at ease with her words...her attitude...her kindness...

"Now stop worrying and go to sleep."

At this, my emotions crossed the finish line. How blessed I was, to be able to stop worrying on command. Knowing her, she probably had no idea about my dreams or the inner workings of my heart, but—

"Adachi," she called softly as she closed her eyes.

—in the end, she always gave me everything I wished for.

"Sleep well."

There was no point in resisting, so I closed my eyes, falling away from this waking dream and sinking into another.

"Sleep well..."

Shimamura.

Silently, I whispered her name.

NAGAFUJI WAS FLOATING in the bathwater, her limbs spread in every direction, naked as the day she was born. Lying on her back, the highest point on her body was her chest. You'd think it'd be her nose, like a normal person, but no. *Damn you, Nagafuji.*

"Must be nice to have a huge bathtub!"

"One of the perks of being rich," I replied absently as I shampooed my hair.

Admittedly, the tub at Nagafuji's house was a relic from the era in which the house was built—which is to say, eons ago—and it was so small, you couldn't even stretch your legs out all the way. The two of us fit inside it just fine when we were kids, but these days it would be impossible. Mostly because of Nagafuji.

"*Ah*, I'm so happy!"

To express her joy, she kicked her feet in the water. The momentum sent her sailing all the way to the side of the tub, where she hit her head and sank like a rock. She was acting like a kid at a ryokan, and I was terrified she was going to try to make this a regular occurrence.

After our bath, we sat on the edge of the porch to cool down. That said, I couldn't exactly "cool down" with Nagafuji pressed right up against me...and yet I couldn't bring myself to scoot away, either.

"Ooh, look at the sky," Nagafuji murmured, slack-jawed. It was the first words she'd spoken since we got out of the tub. "I like windy days. It's easier to see the stars."

"Huh? Oh...yeah, I guess..."

If I had to guess, it was probably the swift movement of the clouds that kept things interesting. Not that Nagafuji was thinking that deeply, of course. She accepted everything in the world at surface value without reading into it, for better or for worse.

"Plus, you guys have a huge yard, so there's lots of greenery to look at. I love this place."

Yet again, she complimented my house. Me personally, though, I was inclined to disagree. If she actually came here often enough for the novelty to wear off, she'd realize just how exhausting it was to live here.

"Nah. I wish my house was as small as yours." That way it wouldn't take so long to get from room to room.

"Wow. You're so greedy."

"Excuse me? If anything, I'm the opposite of greedy! I'm saying I want *less*!"

"Oh. Good point," she shrugged casually, kicking her feet back and forth as they dangled from the porch. "Wanna trade?"

"Ooh. Now there's an idea."

If it was that easy, I'd do it in a heartbeat. And I'd bring all my brothers and maids with me, too. How would a guy like Goushirou handle living at Nagafuji's place? When I tried to picture it, I nearly burst out laughing. Knowing him, he'd probably get a ruler and measure the space between each product on display to make sure it was *just so*. Who knows—maybe he'd actually make a good butcher.

Just then, Nagafuji leaned her body up against me.

"Are...are you bored of looking at the sky or something?"

Then she took my hand...and brought it...*toward her chest*...?!

Silently, my palm pressed against her. Flustered, I stared in shock. She laughed. "I figured I'd let you touch them every now and then, since you like them so much."

"Wh-what?! Now look here, you...!"

"See, aren't I nice? Just don't squeeze, okay?"

Why would I?! I blushed all the way to my ears as I sat there, perfectly still, with my hand against Nagafuji's breast. I couldn't feel much of anything, save for her fingers wrapped around my wrist.

"Having fun?"

"It's really warm." Not just her, but my face, too. *What are we doing right now?* I couldn't even look at her. "Alright, that's enough. Thanks."

Unable to bear it a moment longer, I pulled my hand away. But just then—

"Whoa!"

—Nagafuji grabbed my head and drew it close. Caught off-guard, I collapsed against her chest. Her post-bath warmth made me start sweating all over again.

"Man, what is *up* with you tonight?"

"You're just so cute, Hino!"

She stroked the bath towel between her hand and my hair, almost like I was her beloved pet or something. She was so forward with her compliments... That was what flustered me more than anything. As she ruffled my towel, it felt like I was seeing the real her.

In elementary school, our teachers treated her like a clueless ditz, but when it came down to it, she was just really, really open and honest. Considering she accepted everything at face value, she probably took this stance with her own feelings, too...and I couldn't for the life of me figure out how to counter it. Me, I could never be that open about myself. The most I could do was mask my embarrassment with sarcasm.

"You sure like me a whole bunch, huh?"

"Yup!"

...*At least blush about it a little, would you?*

When I saw the pure, innocent smile on Shimamura's face, I realized: *Oh, this is a dream. Which means I can get away with asking for just about anything, right? Right?*

With this decided, I spread my arms out wide. "Sh-Shimamura! I want a piggyback ride! And headpats! And a big hug! And—"

"Give me a break!"

She smiled awkwardly, and I thought to myself: *Oh god, what if this isn't a dream after all?* But right as I started to freak out, the next thing I knew, I was looking at a darkened ceiling. My heart was pounding a mile a minute. I clutched at my chest.

Brain, please, just let me sleep.

6. Love and Sakura

AS I LAY THERE with my eyes closed, I contemplated how much longer I should pretend to be asleep. I could feel the warm morning sun against my back, but in place of chirping birds, I could only hear Adachi's faint whispers as she prayed:

"Please put me near Shimamura. Please put me near Shimamura."

She sounded so scared and desperate, I wasn't really sure how to react. As you can imagine, I couldn't exactly spring upright like all was well.

Had she prayed that we'd end up in the same class, too? I thought back to the look on her face that day as she leapt for joy. It must have been one of few times that she actually got what she asked for.

I felt her roll over, and then she put her left hand on my almost-completely-numbed right hand. Her fingers slid between mine. It was springtime, and yet her skin was cool to the touch. As we lay there, however, the chill faded away, defeated by my warmth. For some reason, I found I was kind of disappointed to see it go.

I twitched my arm, pretending like I was stirring awake. Instantly, she let go and stopped praying, and I felt her head turn. Then I slowly opened my eyes to find her looking back at me, her lips pursed tightly. Apparently she was afraid of me catching her in the act; her cheeks were as pink as her namesake.

It felt like her face was closer now than it was when we went to bed last night. Her head was cradled in the crook of my elbow, and if either of us had rolled over in our sleep, we would've knocked our foreheads together. *Yikes*. Good thing we were both solid sleepers.

"Good morning."

"G-good...morning..." Adachi stammered, her whole head trembling.

Her eyes were wide open and looked a bit dry, like she'd been up for a while. No surprise there, honestly, given we'd turned in at 8 PM. If anything, I probably overslept. And yet somehow I was *still* sleepy. A small yawn slipped out.

"What happened yesterday?"

Her sudden question confused me. "What?"

"I mean, last night. Did anything...you know...happen?" she asked cryptically. As I stared back in confusion, her face flushed beet-red, all the way to her ears.

"Last night? I'm...kinda not sure what you're talking about. I was asleep...?"

Weren't you literally right there on my arm? Are you feeling okay? Or did something happen without me knowing? Did you doodle on my face or something? Note to self: look in a mirror.

It felt like a question you'd hear in a horror movie, but Adachi's reaction was anything but scared. "Alright then. Okay," she replied, looking sincerely relieved. Then she curled up, closed her damp eyes, and relaxed against my arm like she was thinking about going back to sleep. "Just a dream. Thank god," I was pretty sure I heard her say.

At that point, I couldn't bring myself to shake her awake and ask more questions, so instead I just fell silent. There was a long pause. But unlike on the phone, it wasn't the sort of bottomless abyss that left me feeling trapped. For some reason, the weight against me and the numbness in my arm instilled in me a strange sense of peace. I yawned again, and my fingers twitched.

Did Hino and Nagafuji cuddle in the same bed, too?

I had a vague understanding of their friendship, and yet my own was a mystery.

I turned my head as far as I could manage to look at the clock. It was time to get up and start getting ready for school. Any later and my mom was bound to come knocking. But I couldn't get up unless Adachi got up, and Adachi showed no signs of stirring. Her eyes were still closed.

I moved my arm ever so slightly; her cheeks flushed, and she balled her hand into a fist. Because her complexion was so pale, the most minute color changes were readily obvious. Maybe a tan would help... Summer wasn't that far off, thankfully.

But if we were going to make it to summer, then my first step would be to wake her. I felt guilty, since it was pretty clear she hadn't gotten much sleep, but my only option was to be her alarm clock.

I wiggled my arm vigorously. Adachi shook her head, as if in protest, and clung to my pajamas.

What part of this looks like a "competent student" to you, Mom? God, she's such a needy little baby.

But all I could do was smile and shake my head.

"Hold it, little girl."

Right as we were putting our shoes on in the entryway, my mother flagged me down. *That's one way to address your own daughter, I guess.*

"Take this with you." She handed me a rectangular parcel, then did the same with Adachi. "You, too, Adachi-chan."

I looked down at it and felts its weight. "What *are* these?"

"Take a guess."

"You're...going to make me lunches again?"

"Bingo."

She shot me a thumbs-up. I stared back in surprise. "Where did this come from?"

"Well..." She started to explain, but seemingly decided it was too much work. "Eh, forget it. Just get going already or you'll be late." Then she shooed us out of the house.

What had changed her mind? I looked at Adachi.

She was staring down at her bento box, slack-jawed.

And so we set off on our merry (read: miserable) way to school. As I rode on the back of Adachi's bike, it occurred to me:

"Is this our first time going to school together?"

We'd definitely ridden home together in the past, but this was a first.

Despite the fact that she was steering, Adachi looked up at me. "I think so," she muttered. Then she continued to gaze up at me, so I took it upon myself to watch the road.

Flecks of sunlight scattered through the trees. The stains on the buildings. The flow of vehicles and pedestrians. Long white clouds, streaking across the sky like the sleeves of a blouse. The biting heat of the sunshine against my darkened hair, its warmth somewhere between spring and summer.

Everywhere I looked, it was May.

We passed through the residential district until we reached the road that would lead us to our high school. Under the bright rays of the sun, both beauty and ugliness stood out in sharp relief.

Once Sunday was over, naturally, we were expected to go back to school. And since we were both going to the same place, it made sense for both of us to take Adachi's bike. Her bike was then further weighed down with all of the bags she'd brought for the sleepover, and yet she pedaled as though it was no trouble at all. *What a hard little worker,* I thought to myself half-jokingly. This was not an opinion I often held of her.

"Okay, you need to start paying attention now."

I gave the back of her head a little push. Frowning reluctantly, she tilted her head back down. But right as I moved to pull my hand away, I noticed the faint outlines of a flower pattern embedded in my skin—a vestige of Adachi's weight pressing my arm against the pillow. Was there more hidden under my sleeve? I rubbed my arm through my uniform.

Resting a hand on Adachi's shoulder, I observed her for a moment. Her tension was visible, not through her expression, but through her white-knuckled grip on the handlebars. After all, we—or at least, she—had a big event coming up today: the seating shuffle. No longer would we be organized alphabetically by last name.

Did her prayers help her face reality? Was there a point to just sitting around and thinking instead of taking action? Either way, I was looking forward to the outcome.

On the day of the entrance ceremony, the sakura blossoms had just started to fall. Today, there was no trace of them left.

Had I ever been fully conscious of the sakura blossoms before now? I pondered this to myself as I walked toward the school building, occasionally looking up at the sky. Whenever spring break came to an end, my attention would inevitably be drawn to the piles of petals covering the ground... Perhaps I'd never actually seen a sakura tree in full bloom before.

Of course, now that I was thinking about it, I suddenly felt the desire to correct this, but I couldn't exactly turn back time. How many more chances would I have to see the blossoms?

"Hmm..."

I looked from the scrap of paper in my hand to the numbers written on the chalkboard. Apparently the seating shuffle had started at some point while I was lost in thought. My homeroom teacher's system was as follows: Each of us, in alphabetical order, would reach into a bowl and draw a scrap of paper with a number on it. Then we'd look at the chalkboard, find the corresponding desk, and move to it.

Adachi had already finished moving desks; I could feel her gaze lingering on my back.

Ultimately, I ended up moving one column to the left, second row from the back. As for Adachi, she was now three desks to my right.

"Well, that didn't change much..."

We weren't especially close, but neither were we on opposite sides of the room. Sure, we were in the same row, but we were still three columns apart, so it was hard to say how successful her prayer really was.

As the seating shuffle continued noisily, I put my chin in my hand and looked over at Adachi. Our eyes met. Her expression was as stoic as ever, but she wasn't staring down at her hands, so she seemed to be in decent spirits. She looked back at me, her gaze swimming unsteadily, the same way it had when we woke up. In other words, she was sleepy. *Poor thing. Hang in there, kiddo,* I thought dryly.

Later, during class, I looked over and made eye contact with Adachi. She held my gaze for a moment, then hastily looked away, as if she couldn't take it anymore. But I kept looking at her anyway, and sure enough, she glanced over at me again. Somehow, no matter how many heads were in our way, we always managed to find each other.

Then she turned away and stared down at her textbook, wide-eyed, tracing a finger over its pages. But I knew her well enough to know that she wasn't really reading it. The flower hairpin swayed with her unstable movements.

Smiling, I looked over at the bright sunlight streaming in through the windows.

It's May, alright.

One minute it was the first day of our second year, and then I blinked, and a whole month flew by. My high school career only had one more April left. Then one more May, then one more June. Today would never happen again. There was no retry button in real life. And as time sped by faster and faster, I became painfully conscious of this fact. I couldn't spend my whole life taking it easy.

Perhaps the sakura blossoms were symbolic of my lost time, slowly slipping away petal by petal.

Adachi was keenly aware that her time was limited, which was why she spent every day in what appeared to be a constant struggle to live her life to the fullest...or was I overestimating her?

Though she appeared to nearly nod off at several points, she never completely fell asleep. She was putting up a valiant effort, and it made me smile. Like the faint warmth of spring, it took the weight off my shoulders. And now that I was able to breathe again, I realized—

Someday...I couldn't be certain when exactly, but I knew it would happen eventually...someday in the future, when there were no more spring breaks to be had, and my high school friends were a distant memory...someday I would have to spend sakura season alone. But until then, perhaps it couldn't hurt to enjoy the blossoms while they were around. It might even be fun.

April was over, and the blossoms were no longer blooming...but if I ever wanted to see Sakura, she was only three desks away.

Afterword

ARGENTO SOMA! Buy it today on DVD!

Did you know I have a banana allergy? I'm *wholly* unable to eat a whole banana. Apparently I can't have kiwi, either—anyway, hello. Oh, and I can't have pineapple—anyway, hi there. It would appear that these tropical fruits hate my guts. Farewell, Tahiti. Not that I've ever been.

So, that was Volume 4 of *Adachi and Shimamura*. Kind of wild that it's lasted this long, huh? My main problem with writing a long series is that I never know what to do with repeat holidays. It feels kind of silly to do Valentine's and Christmas stories all over again. How do they handle this in manga? These are the kinds of things I thought about while I wrote this volume. Thank you for buying my book.

For some reason my fingers always smell like chlorine. This is a thought I just had while sniffing my hand.

Another thing: Recently I've been thinking...I don't trust anyone who says they control how much effort they put in based on the job. Like, I don't care what kind of work it is—if you're getting paid to do it, then give it everything you've got and don't slack off. That kind of thing. That's what I'd like to see in an ideal world. That said, I don't know how you'd "slack off" writing a novel, anyway.

At the current time of writing, I've been playing *Kenka Bancho 6*. And each year, as I struggle to remember enough math to pass my finals, I can tell I'm getting old. Oh, and I played *Ukiyo no Shishi* and *Ukiyo no Roushi*. Samurai swordfighting games are a rare and valuable commodity, and I enjoyed my time with them. I just wish they'd give me the option to use the same katana stance and sheath animations that the NPCs get.

That reminds me—at an autograph session in 2014, one particular fan was passionately trying to convince me to send the girls to the hot springs. But is going to the hot springs something that teenage girls would realistically do for fun? Granted, I've read a manga where some junior high students went, but high school...?

Thank you to my editors: M, A, and O. I couldn't have published this book on my own, and your assistance was invaluable, so I'm extremely grateful. Oh, and thank you to Non-san for the illustrations.

See, I was always a good kid, and when you asked me who I respected most of all, I would always write "my parents"—until junior high, at least. But when I see my father eating veggies and taking medicine at the same time, it gives me pause.

Not sure if there will be more volumes in the future, but if so, I hope you'll continue to show your support.

—Hitoma Iruma

Experience these great light**novel** titles from Seven Seas Entertainment

See the complete Seven Seas novel collection at
sevenseaslightnovel.com